Also by John Darnielle

Black Sabbath's Master of Reality (33⅓)

Wolf in White Van

Wolf in White Van

John Darnielle

HarperCollins*Publishers*Ltd

Wolf in White Van
Copyright © 2014 by John Darnielle.
All rights reserved.

Published by HarperCollins Publishers Ltd,
by arrangement with Farrar, Straus and Giroux, LLC

First Canadian edition

HarperCollins books may be purchased for educational, business,
or sales promotional use through our Special Markets Department.

HarperCollins Publishers Ltd
2 Bloor Street East, 20th Floor
Toronto, Ontario, Canada
M4W 1A8

www.harpercollins.ca

Library and Archives Canada Cataloguing in Publication
information is available upon request.

ISBN 978-1-44343-738-7

Printed and bound in the United States of America
RRD 9 8 7 6 5 4 3 2

*To my early teachers—Debbie Vancil, Terry Kneisler,
Rosemary Adam—true guardians of the Trace*

"And the treasure?" I broke in eagerly.

He laughed in savage self-mockery.

"There was no gold there, no precious gems— nothing"—he hesitated—"nothing that I could bring away."

—Robert E. Howard, "The Thing on the Roof"

One

I My father used to carry me down the hall to my room after I came home from the hospital. By then I could walk if I had to, but the risk of falling was too great, so he carried me like a child. It's a cluster memory now: it consists of every time it happened and is recalled in a continuous loop. He did it every day, for a long time, from my first day back until what seemed like a hundred years later, and after a while, the scene blurred into innumerable interchangeable identical scenes layered one on top of the other like transparencies. On the wall to the right, as you head toward my room, there's a small bookcase with a painting above it, a western scene: hills and trees, a lake. A blue and green vista near sundown, a silent place. But if you look harder, or happen to turn your head at the right moment as you pass, you see figures, human figures, on what you might otherwise take for an empty ridge. It's like an optical illusion, this hunting party on the near hill, their curving hats dark in the orange dusk: they come out of hiding if you look at the empty scenery long enough. They were always there in my journey, popping up in the same place each time I'd drift by in my half-sleep. They never lost their power to surprise just by being there, a little smoke rising from somewhere within their three-strong party, their brushstroke rifles resting lightly on their shoulders.

Next to the bookcase, receding into the wall, there's a chest-high shelf for a rotary phone. To the left, just past the painting, on the other side of the hall, is the bathroom, the sort of open door that if the cameras found it as they passed through the house in a horror movie would trigger a blast of synthesizers. In my many days home after the hospital, I spent long hours in there, lifetimes: in the tub, at the sink. Just getting in and out. It would be a long time before I could comfortably stand underneath a showerhead, and my parents didn't trust me to sit in the bathtub by myself, so the bathroom became a communal space of forced intimacy. Reconstructed skin is very sensitive to temperature and moisture; the pain sneaks up on you. Every other day they'd bathe me, and every time, I'd feel like it wasn't so bad for a few minutes; and then the heat would slacken the resewn flaps of my cheeks a little, and the tingling would start up, a rippling alarm traveling down confused wires. I was too generally exhausted to be able to experience fear or panic for longer than a moment, and I'd try to bear the feeling evenly, but its grip was hard and sure, and it held me. My parents' eyes on me, trying to head off the pain at the pass, to start hoisting me out before I had to ask. Several kinds of pain for several people. The portal still glows with menace in my memory.

Ahead and beyond, two further doors: mine, straight on, and to the right, my parents'. My parents' room is an uncataloged planet, a night sky presence unknown to scientists but feared by the secret faithful who trade rumors of its mystery.

I stood before this door once and didn't go in: that's the extent of the legend, really, but my journey down the hall that night, down the same stream through which my father carries me now in my wheeling memory, hints at pockets in the story that are still obscure, which will never find light. What if I'd gone in? I didn't go in. I stood there a minute and then turned away. If I'd turned around: What then? There are several possibilities; they open onto their own clusters of new ones, and there's an end somewhere, I'm sure, but I'll never see it.

I feel and remember my father's arms underneath me when I've come home from the hospital; he isn't strong enough to do this, but he is forcing himself to do it; I am heavy in his arms, and I feel safe there, but I am lost, and I need constantly to be shoring up the wall that holds my emotions at bay, or I will feel something too great to contain. I see the painting, those cowboy huntsmen at dusk, and they surprise me a little, and I feel my breath catch in my chest when I scan the bathroom; and then I arc my great head a little to the right toward my parents' room, which disappears from view as my father nudges at the base of my bedroom door with his foot and then turns jaggedly on his heels so we'll both fit through the frame. He lowers me onto my new bed, the one from the hospital-supply place on White, and I feel the hot egg crate mattress underneath the sheet. Dad squeezes my hand like I remember him doing when I was very small. We look at each other. Teamwork. This happens several times a day, or it's a single thing that's always happening somewhere, a current into which I can slip when I need to remember something.

I saw this kid playing on the big metal wheel with the soldered piping: the merry-go-round. The merry-go-round at the fair is for babies, but the playground kind can throw you into the air at high speed; they have to put wood chips around it to break your fall just in case. This happened twice while I was watching: the kid spun the wheel faster and faster, jumped on, tried to crawl in to the still hub and lost his footing, and ended up sailing into the air and coming down hard. He'd lie there and laugh, dizzy, and then punch reset on the whole scene.

At my grandparents' place, after the last fish went missing, they filled the pond in with cedar chips: I used to play out there when I was little. It was a half-hidden spot between the house and the garage, too small a space to think of as a yard—three cypresses, some rocks here and there, and the former pond. I remember the changeover from water to wood, the shift in tone: that was how I ended up conjuring the place now. I lived whole lives out there back then.

The day they drained the pond I'd gone out back by myself after dinner. This had been a lakeside clearing in a forest for me, a magic place of wizards and wandering knights. It was still magic without the water, but the magic was different now. I could sense it. I closed my eyes.

When I opened them, I felt my mind working transformations. No lake but a cave floor. Not trees but torches burning with a mystic light. Behind them: the back wall of a cave. Before them, me, enthroned, my regal seat hewn from ancient rock, immovable, imperious.

The throne was actually a single stone brought in by the crew that filled in the pond. But under the weight of my small body, I felt it sprout ornately decorated arms with claws at the ends, and a bejeweled latticework back that climbed up several feet above my head. Transformed, it now boasted four short, sturdy legs that terminated in great glowing orbs pressing hard into the earth beneath. I took control of the place, of the scene: I made it mine. Groans echoed in the cave. Brittle bones broke beneath the knees of my crawling subjects. We had moved from San Jose to Montclair a few months back; it had ruined something for me, I was having a hard time making new friends. I had grown receptive to dark dreams.

I saw animal skins running down the cave floor, skull dust rising. Everyone in my orbit would have a terrible day: the arbiter of days had decreed it. From my increasingly improbable perch I looked toward the dark heavens somewhere up beyond the imagined cave ceiling, and I pantomimed the aspect of a man thinking hard about what he might want to eat. And then I looked back down to the present moment, and I spoke; "I am King Conan," I said. "I thirst for blood."

Backyard Conan, thrown together from half-understood comic books only, took several liberties with the particulars. The Conan that the world knew didn't drink blood, wasn't ruthless and cold. In his original form, he'd lived to follow a warrior's code of honor: enemies met death at his sword, and fellow barbarians shared in the plunder, but they were all men who lived by a code. The code was cruel, but just, consistent: coherent. When I became Conan things were different; his new birth had left scars. I ruled a smoking, wrecked kingdom with a hard and deadly hand. It was dark and gory. No one liked living there, not even its king. It had a soundtrack. All screams.

7

Small for my age, pants still too tight, enthroned atop the lone rock near the drained pond now stuffed with cedar, I looked out into green leaves drifting down and sought the far distance. In came men carrying prisoners, their hands and ankles tied to branches like hogs at a Hawaiian feast. They were yelling in unknown tongues. Their muscles strained. The fire pit before my throne had sprung up in full glaze. The screams of the condemned ascended to the stars.

I couldn't fill in the finer points of the plot: what anybody'd done wrong, why they had to die. It didn't matter. I opened my mouth like a great bird. I was coming down to deal death: to the guilty, to the innocent, to anyone within reach. To *you*, before me, trapped in the cave above the fire. Flayed and roasted and shared out among the nameless. To die screaming reduced to smoke. Lost in some kingdom found by accident and never heard from again in this world. Eaten by forgotten warriors on unremembered quests for plunder now lost forever.

I was in the park feeding squirrels when the memory crested, peeking out from behind a sort of interior immovable monument in my skull where all the old things lie. I couldn't put an exact date to it. Somewhere late in the early game, among the several moves from one house to another, my dad between jobs and trying to find his footing. The filled-in fish pond seemed like a giveaway, but it could also have been flown in from some other scene, pasted on. Still: it grew vivid. The ivy in the backyard turning to jungle vines. The ground parching itself, bleaching itself. The composite sky—Pismo, Montclair, San Jose, places we'd lived, lost transitions—cracking along its surface like an old painting in an abandoned museum. And me, in the middle, on a throne whose legs eventually solidified as human femurs bound together with thick rope. I spent several minutes in deep concentration trying to get the picture fixed, to spot clues that would give me some exact sense of when and where, but the edges kept blurring. Sometimes I have trouble finding the edges.

Presently the kid from the merry-go-round turned up in front of me—I'd gotten distracted by the squirrels while remembering my childhood, and I ended up lost. When I looked up, there he was—five years old, I figured, possibly younger. I used to be good at guessing things. I'm not now. He sat down next to me, a little distance between us, and his eyes went from my face to my hand, still casting out peanuts for squirrels or blue jays one at a time. And then he brought his gaze back to my face, where it rested.

He was very quiet as he looked up at me: I was a kid once; I thought I recognized on this one the look of a child deliberating within himself. He pointed in the direction of his question when he finally said it: "What did you do to your face?"

Well, I told him all about it. He listened while I spoke, while I explained what I had done, and when, and how, and he nodded at all the right places in the story. And then, of course, when I was done explaining, he asked "Why?" which is a tricky question for me, since the correct answer is "I don't know": and that's a hard thing to say once all the cards are right there on the table. But he pressed me on it: "Yes you do," he said. "You do so know."

It was a surprising moment on a day I'd set aside for doing

very little, in what I'd already begun to think of as the aftermath. When I'd gotten into the car to drive to the park, I'd thought to myself: You've earned an empty moment or two. Instead, here we were. I thought how there's always more to something than I usually think there is, and I said then that he was right; that I was the only one who could know why I had done what I did, and that I couldn't think of anybody else who'd be able to come up with any kind of answer. But it was still true that I didn't have any "why" for him; I just didn't have one. I had looked for one, and it wasn't there.

I could see him starting to think, hard, during the little minute of quiet that followed. Wheels turning. I wondered if maybe something difficult was opening itself up to him— that maybe people do things for no reason, that things just happen, that nobody really knows much.

"I don't believe you. You don't know," he said. He looked straight at me. "You are a fibber."

"Am I a fibber?" I said, smiling, even though I feel ugly when I smile. I feel like I might have been good with children in a different life.

He nodded his head fiercely. "You are!"

I flipped my hands palms up, hip level at either side, sitting there on what I now thought of as our bench, and I shrugged. Inside my head I could see how I might have looked to some observer standing at a few paces, me and this kid pointing, and my face; and how we might again look to another observer, stationed at some slightly greater distance. To somebody waiting at the light across the street. How we'd look on film. Or from space. In a Kodak frame. All these ways.

And I liked what I saw, when I took it all in. It was ridiculous. It had an air of the inevitable to it. My smile got bigger as I let the picture grow to occupy the fullness of the space inside my head, and I just let it happen, even though I know it looks awful. Too late to hold back now. I looked over at the kid's family, who were motioning for him to return to their fold, and I felt something inside, something fine and small and dense. I looked out across the park. Came all this way and now here I am.

At the apartment complex the Saturday gardeners were just finishing up. The grass was tight and clean. They'd trimmed back the gardenia hedge so severely in some places that the stalks looked like petrified bones, little hands reaching up from the earth.

I went inside and I puttered around on the computer, try-ing to finish up something I'd been working on, a little corner of a detour hardly anybody ever cared about. Most weekends I try to put my work aside, but there wasn't anything else to do. Then I checked my bank accounts, a nervous habit: I'm not rich, or even that comfortable, but my grandmother opened up a savings account for me after my accident, and she kept put-ting a little into it every month for ten years until she died. It's a security blanket now. I look at what's in there whenever I start to worry that my own savings or the insurance payments or my work won't be enough. It's like checking a lock on a door: just making sure no bad guys are going to get in. And then I played some music, old music, and it sounded awful, and I loved it, I loved it so much.

Later, the nurse from the VNA came by for my sinus

irrigation and let herself in—it was Vicky, who I always call "Victory," because usually by the time she shows up I need a nurse so bad that I can barely breathe. "Victory!" I'll say then, raising my weak arms up champion-style. I sound hilarious when I try to pronounce the letter *r*.

"Well, Sean, yes, Victory's here. Victory's here, all right," she said today, the way she does, responding to things she hears as if they were thoughts that occurred to her inside her head, volume dwindling as she goes, the folds of her neck shaking gently. She looked at me, taking stock. "And Sean's here, too. Sean's here, right? Just like always. How you doing?"

And I started to say "fine," and I meant to say "fine," but I ended up saying that I felt my life was filled like a big jug to the brim with almost indescribable joy, so much that I hardly knew how to handle it. That was how I put it, what I said: "I feel like my life is filled," and then all the rest of it, one big exhale. I am not an eloquent person, and I was surprised to hear myself talking like that, but only a little surprised, because it was exactly the feeling I had in my heart. It was right there at the surface waiting to come out. No way of counting my blessings. No way for anyone to count that high. And so Vicky told me that Jesus always makes a Way, which is how visiting nurses often talk, I've found over the years, and I said yes, yes, yes that's true, yes that certainly is true.

2 I. THE BRIDGE

Reactor five, visible from S.R. 60 just past the Grove Avenue exit, was collapsing. Radiation sickness traveled on poison winds through the tract home neighborhoods; within a few weeks, most in the region were too sick to work, and within a few months over half of them were dead. Neighboring counties began raiding the afflicted region for supplies; the contaminated goods they brought back served as mobile hosts for the burgeoning mutation. The age of empire had entered into the first gasps of its terminal phase.

Radiation levels were so high in the bodies of even the most tenacious survivors that total contamination below the 36th parallel north seemed unavoidable. People fled in terror, seeking food and shelter to the west and east. Basal ganglia calcified in the stricken; the streets rang at night with the screams of the lost. Northern movement remained blocked; the armies of the north, formed overnight and bonded by fear, stood prepared to fight until the last of their numbers fell.

In Missouri, fifty California delegates to the Southern Baptist Convention in Kansas City were housed at a Holiday Inn near the freeway. The convention was first delayed, then canceled, when the gravity of the situation on reactor five became clear; the aggrieved were told to return to their families, to save what they could. There was to be no return home. Disorder and panic spread like brushfire. Uncontaminated cities quickly formed citizen posses, built strong walls around their boundaries, and guarded them with heavy armor. Three of the Kansas City fifty set out in a southerly course tending westward, despite misgivings. Their eventual ends are unknown.

The remaining members of the delegation left Missouri on foot for the fallow fields of Kansas. Among their numbers were several laymen, employees on reactor five. Historians posit that genetic contamination among employees at the reactor would have been at or near 100 percent by the time of the collapse, though this is conjecture. Only two verifiable employees of the reactor are known to have survived the ensuing chaos of the days that followed. They were in Kansas City on the day the core melted, and are remembered now as the first people, ten years later, to be denied entrance to the Trace Italian.

For the third time since sunrise you see men in gas masks sweeping the highway. It's dusk. They are approaching the overpass where you hide in the weeds. You can only guess, but guesses are better than nothing: you calculate your chances of escaping unnoticed at 15 percent. When the nearest of them is close enough for you to hear the sound of the gravel underneath his yellow rubber boots, you know that the time has come for you to act.

Welcome to Trace Italian, a game of strategy and survival! You may now make your first move.

Within earshot of my twitching, living body I heard them tell my parents I wasn't going to last long. That was, almost to a phrase, how they put it: "We don't expect patients in Sean's condition to last long." I was too febrile to take offense or to feel relieved; the words just floated past my consciousness like a scrolling news bulletin at the bottom of the screen during a baseball game. Wherever it was my conscious self had actually fled to, the terrain lay somewhere out beyond where you might wonder what people mean by the things they say. I was having dreams of a guy named Marco, who was the editor and publisher of a small-press horror magazine called *Marco*. He was talking to me through the tight oval mouth hole of his ski mask.

He had all kinds of interesting things to say. He kept picking at his teeth with a steel toothpick, and I wanted to ask him where you get a steel toothpick from, but then I'd bubble up to the bright surface again and hear the chatter and see all the people and their hospital machines, like the world coming into total focus when you first wake up; and then Marco, whose hidden face probably originated in trailers for spy movies and send-two-dollars-for-our-illustrated-catalog ads in magazines or on the backs of comic books, would go wobbly like the vertical hold on a TV and vanish.

Still, even after he'd disappeared from my visual field, I could make out his voice, trying to fight its way back into the world of the living, wriggling out over the bells and the beeps and the people talking past one another. In the hall on the other side of the curtain, my mom kept describing the tableau in my bedroom, going over the details of it with the nurse and the treatment team. The louder she got the louder Marco had to speak to be heard; he also had to compete with the patient in the bay next to mine, who was screaming. After a few passes it started to seem like Marco only spoke when my coherence dropped, and got clearer when I let the fever take me: as soon as I'd start to lose my grip on things, he'd come suddenly through. When the fever settled in for a long swell, he coached me quickly up from my bed, and he hustled me through the door while everybody's back was turned. From there we went speedily down the sterile busy hallways and hurried through a door that opened onto an eerie desert landscape, all cactus and cow skulls and shaky gravity. The scene played itself out several times, finding its bearings, but then someone from the outside would touch my hand, or say something that breeched the bur-bling static, and I'd hear the real things around me, my family and the doctors and the constant low hum of the building.

I think it was our third trip down the hallway that took me deepest into the desert; I remember that suddenly it was night out there, and that there was a huge, deep drone in the air, and a trillion stars. I remember Marco in the full flower of his clarity, asking me questions, but I could only tell that they were questions by the rising tone he'd end them on. The ac-tual words were heavily distorted, movie dialogue through a blown speaker or a fading radio signal turned up way too loud. Atop a low butte in the near distance I saw his armies gath-ered, the incomprehensible force of his voice somehow in-creasing their strength, maybe even their numbers. He began to tower over me in stature, quickly, and before long the masked boy my age who'd guided me out of the emergency room a moment before had become a giant, nine or ten feet tall, skinny and spindly, his voice threading through the desert hum like an insect song. I listened for some opening in his monologue where I might cut in and ask what was going on, and I prepared myself to get in one good question before his squadrons came charging down the hill. He had grabbed hold of my neck like I was a puppy; he was lifting me into the air. But just then someone started applying silver sulfadiazine to my forehead, and it burned, and I snapped back into my surroundings.

The whole thing only lasted for a few minutes, and I seldom thought of it again except to try and figure it out: where it came from, I mean. Because there isn't any magazine called *Marco*, and anyone connected with the magazine *Marco* is a phantom construction that my mind scared up during the first few minutes after the disaster.

The art therapist came in fairly early on, or what feels now like it must have been fairly early on. I was in no condition. I was running a temperature they couldn't figure out; it came and went. But I was awake some of the time, and that was enough. She stuck to simple questions: "Do you like to paint?"

"Not really."

"Puzzles?"

"Sometimes."

"Do you like to draw?"

"Yes."

"Good! What kinds of things do you like to draw?"

I looked up to where I'd been looking, where I'd still be

looking long after she left. I felt warm. "The universe," I said, with a little effort.

People have ideas and theories about coping with catastrophic injury, but most of them are based in practicalities. They're right in thinking that the practicalities—how will you live? what will you do?—are important, but these aren't the main thing. The main thing is what happens to your vision, how you're a little different after you've seen a few things, and as far as I know, nobody really gets this, though I thought Chris Haynes did once. Something in his overall distrust of the path going forward felt moored to some bigger thing I knew about, something he'd either inferred from the play or known instinctively. But maybe not. It's hard to say.

One way of coping, anyway, is to stare at the ceiling. A hospital room ceiling, white, like an egg in a carton that's been in the refrigerator for several weeks, away from the light, is dull, completely uniform, revealing variations only when you stare at the same spot for some time and then, very slowly, venture out. If you concentrate hard enough on the task, you might find a bubble or grain where a brush or a roller has stopped to reverse its stroke. You could let your attention rest there for a while; you could imagine the future of the ceiling, the battles playing out up there, camps pitched when the building was new back in unremembered time. You could picture the paint beginning to crack and fragment, and see, either in your mind's eye or out there on the actual field of play if your vision spreads that far, the plaster underneath it learning to follow the cracks, the mildew forming on residues left by cleaning solutions beginning to breed, and colonies of microscopic life-forms, hostile to dull matter, developing their ruthless, mindless strategy: consume, reproduce, survive. You can see the hospital when the building has been emptied of patients but a few workers remain: administrators, janitors, members of the demolition crew. You can see the ceiling in the next room, following the splits of the ceiling in its neighbor, and the one beyond that in turn, and then the greater canvas, the sky at night gone flat and painted white, the constellations in the cracking paint, the dust the cracks bring into being as they form, finding free land where none had been before their coming.

Nurses and doctors come and go, and family. It's like they're visiting a person at his lonely outpost on the space station, miles above the earth. How do they get there—just coming in through the door like that? In the brief moment between infinite communion with the ceiling and the beginning of whatever conversation they've come to strike up, it seems like the deepest mystery in the world. And then they break the spell, and the world contracts, palpably shifts from one reality into a new and much more unpleasant one, in which there is pain, and suffering, and people who when they are hurt stay hurt for a long time or sometimes forever, if there is such a thing as forever. Forever is a question you start asking when you look at the ceiling. It becomes a word you hear in the same way that people who associate sound with color might hear a flat sky-blue. The open sky through which forgotten satellites travel. Forever.

So when I remember the ceiling I try to invest it with meaning somehow. I try to connect its cracks and bubbles to palpable things out there in the world, to things I might have run across later. I treat the imperfections like tea leaves. I remember it as vividly as I can, and I look for shapes in things too small to have any visible shape, and I see centaurs or cavemen or trowels or piles of bricks, and I try to draw lines between the shapes and the slow sweet life I built for myself when I finally got out and learned I wasn't, thank God, welcome at home anymore. But eventually I locate what I'd known I'd find up there all along, what I'd been seeing already in brief seconds of lucidity arising from the murk of those nights become days and those days of no light. I see my own face. I see it as it was, preserved in stray signals too late to read right.

I'm pretty sure that's the lesson there was to learn in the hospital: the main one. And I'm pretty sure my play was the right one to make. Because the unnamed every-player who lies in the weeds at the moment of Trace Italian's opening move— that's me. It's me. Motionless, ready for something, awake and aware. When the player gets up from the weeds, as he or she always does, because the first move is rigged and all players arrive persuaded that they must act, everything changes: He enters a world where danger's everywhere. He has a goal now, something to do with his life. His map is marked; he's headed somewhere as he rides down the desolate plain.

But this is the point where we split, the player and I. He heads for the road to seek shelter or something to eat. But I remain in the stasis of the opening scene, bits of gravel sticking to my face, cold night coming on. I am strong enough to endure it. I am strong enough to remain in its arms forever. I won't get up; I have seen the interior once. I'm not going back.

One thing I've learned is it's better sometimes, in the weeds, to resist the temptation to stand up and follow the compass.

Years later when they made me look at pictures of Lance and Carrie I remembered Marco, the empty, incoherent prophecy I'd heard amid the chaos. For a second, as I flipped through the evidence, my long-forgotten hallucination became real, and I wondered how he'd managed to remain hidden for so long. What if I'd tried to talk to the doctors about him; why hadn't my mind offered him up as a way to get them off my back? I'd had plenty of encouragement. "Who made you do this, Sean?" my father asked at my bedside, my hand in his. I thought then how nice it would have been to have a good answer ready to give to him, a little gift from son to father, something he could take to his friends by way of explanation. To blame Marco. To lay it at his feet.

"Have you seen these people before?" the attorney asked me in the conference room, running through the planned stations of his performance, giving Carrie's parents their money's worth. He fanned several photographs across the table in front of me and waited for my reply. But they were impossible to understand, all of them and each of them; they belonged to a context that couldn't be referenced outside of itself, incredibly important in one way and completely meaningless in another. They were artists' renditions of somebody's dream. What could I say? Sure I have, a long time ago. You wouldn't understand.

3 There are games I'm prouder of than Trace Italian but it doesn't really matter how I feel. Trace Italian is what built Focus Games, and if people know my name at all, Trace Italian is why they know it. It was my first idea; they say your first ideas are your best ones. I think it's maybe dangerous to think that way all the time. But when I remember finally building Trace Italian, seeing how it was actually going to come together and really work, then I know what people mean about their first ideas being the best. There is something fierce and starved about first ideas.

I'd harbored the Trace concept for a long time—I think I was inspired by a commercial for an old board game called Stay Alive. It starred a bunch of kids playing on a beach; there were no adults around, and waves crashed angrily against rock cliffs nearby. The children pushed or pulled levers on a playfield, opening holes in the board as they did so; eventually all marbles on the board except one would drop out of play, and then the winner would announce, in a breathless voice that suggested he couldn't believe his luck: "I'm the sole survivor!" It held my attention. As a child I wanted everything to be in some way concerned with endings. The end of the world. The last Neanderthal. The final victim. The stroke of midnight. So children playing a game called Stay Alive on a beach with nobody else around, that spoke to something in me, something I'd maybe been born with. Of the many logos for imaginary products I would come to design throughout high school, Trace Italian was the first. I'd gotten the name from dry days in history class during a lesson on medieval fortifications: anything that involved the word *star* always sounded like it was speaking directly to me. The *trace italienne* involved triangular defensive barricades branching out around all sides of a fort: stars within stars within stars, visible from space, one layer of protection in front of another for miles. The *World Book* preferred the term *star fort*, which I also liked, but in idly guessworking *trace italienne* into English I'd stumbled across a phrase that had, for me, an autohypnotic effect. TRACE ITALIAN. I would spend hours writing and rewriting the name in stylized block capitals, reticulated line segments forming letters like the readout on a calculator. On notebook paper rubbed raw with erasures, the evolving logo resembled a department store's name spelled out in dots and dashes on cash register tape: RILEYS UNIVERSITY SQUARE. The driving image for my game involved people running for shelter across a scorched planet. There was something on fire in the near distance behind them. Their faces looked out from the page toward their goal. The Trace Italian represented shelter, and it was shaped like a star. That was all I had.

It was later, lying supine and blind for days, faced with the choice of either inventing internal worlds or having no world at all to inhabit, when I started to fill in the details: how the

23

planet had been ruined (reactor five); how the cities had been emptied (mutant hominids from sea caves seeking out coastal cities for uncontaminated flesh, and continuing to move inland, spreading disease and killing innocents); where and how the surviving humans had built the Trace Italian (far inland, with their bare hands, from available materials cut and tumbled and hewn and polished over generations for several hundred years). How it rose from the landscape, bigger than its medieval counterparts, a shining structure on the plains, protecting the sprawling self-contained city underneath it, a barrier against the outside world and a sign to would-be intruders that its architects were people of great vision and design. Thinking of games as a way to kill time in history class had been one thing, but filling out the map and telling the story of every spot on it by myself, in my head, on my back: it was a refuge for me. I identified with the people I'd created to populate the barren landscape. I shared their goal: to find the location of the Trace Italian. Work through the ant-leg limbs of the star layer by layer until you find the shining heart. Get there at last. Stay there.

I identified with the seekers to the point of imagining myself as one among their numbers. Pushing myself against the wall-rail down the hall to the shower room, I would picture myself scurrying shirtless through the few gutted buildings that remained in the slumping cities, whistling signals to the others who crawled across the crossbeams; served lunch, I would imagine that I was foraging for untainted canned foods, coughing through dust that rose from the shelves of a grocery store on an empty block in a long-depopulated city. Lying in my bed, I would think: I have been wounded en route to the

24

Trace Italian. I am going to have to heal myself, or limp to safety. Get up. Get up. Get up.

One day one of the nurses caught me sketching a dungeon, one of the innumerable and potentially terminal signal stops on the road to the star fort, and she looked at it over the side-rail for some time, scrunching up her brow. I could feel her, scrutinizing my work, her eyes following the spindly arms of a mutated star, and then looking at my face as my undistracted bandaged hands determinedly cornered right angle after right angle. I knew she wanted to ask what I was doing, but I had the advantage. Nobody liked to see me speak.

The way you play Trace Italian seems almost unbearably quaint from a modern perspective, and people usually don't believe me when I tell them it's how I supplement my monthly insurance checks, but people underestimate just how starved everybody is for some magic pathway back into childhood. Trace Italian is a mail-based game. A person sees a small ad for it in the back pages of *Analog* or *The Magazine of Fantasy and Science Fiction*—maybe he sees the ad month after month for ages—and then one day he gets bored and sends a self-addressed stamped envelope to Focus Games, and I send him back an explanatory brochure. The brochure gives a brief but vivid sketch of the game's imagined environment—no pictures, just words—and explains the basic mechanics of play: a trial subscription buys you four moves through the first dungeons, and five dollars a month plus four first-class postage stamps keep a subscription current. I boil down handwritten, sometimes lengthy paragraphs that players send me to simple choices—does this mean *go through the door*, or *continue down the road*?—and then I select the corresponding three-page scenario from a file, scribble a few personalized lines at the bottom, and stuff it into an envelope. They respond with more paragraphs, sometimes pages, describing how they move in reaction to where they've landed. Eventually they recognize the turns they've taken as segments of a path that can belong only to them.

A player's first move isn't necessarily the truest or clearest view of that person I'll get, but it's often the most naked, because it takes a while to situate yourself within an imaginary landscape. When you respond to the initial subscriber packet with your opening move—when you come to the bridge—you haven't had a chance to get much sense of the game's rhythms, so you're awkward, halting, more likely to overplay your hand. The open path at the overpass gives way to grand schemes, huge, multipart responses, whole narratives from within the canvas newly forming inside the player's imagination. I keep myself out of it; I interpret and react, like a flowchart responding flatly to a person who's asking it how to live.

I did it this way for years, mechanically helping people through the chambers of my original hospital vision, occasionally even typing out fresh moves one page at a time on an IBM Selectric, my face hot with bandages, the work distracting me from my circumstances. The advent of the internet looked like it would kill off the game, and I wondered what I'd do for work, but people will surprise you. By 2003—long after most of the magazines that had served as initial points of entry had stopped publishing, the few left displaying my ads to fewer and fewer subscribers—the number of dedicated players had risen to the mid-hundreds, none of whom were at all interested in shifting their daily play over to video games or MMORPGs. My rate had risen with the times, to ten dollars a month. There were websites that scanned and posted as many moves as they could collect, but not many people interested in seeing the moves out of turn: the point was the play. And beyond all that, plenty of people had been involved too long to turn back. Their quiet fervor attracted a few new curious seekers each month, and the replacement rate was more or less constant—people sometimes grew out of the game or got frustrated with their progress, but a few more always came along to take their place. The core was committed. Their minds were made up. They meant to reach the Trace Italian. They thirsted for the security it offered, for the sanctuary of the interior.

The inside of the Trace Italian, of course, does not exist. A player can get close enough to see it: it shines in the new deserts of Kansas, gleaming in the sun or starkly rising from the winter cold. The rock walls that protect it meet in points around it, one giving way to another, for days on end. But the dungeons into which you'll fall as you work through the pathways to its gates number in the low hundreds, and if you actually get into the entry hall, there are a few hundred more sub-dungeons before you'll actually reach somewhere that's truly safe. Technically, it's possible to get to the last room in the final chamber of the Trace Italian, but no one will ever do it. No one will ever live that long.

I opened about a dozen envelopes today; the process has been the same for years. First, I open as many as I think I can take care of in one sitting. Then I stack them on the floor by the desk, letters and SASEs still inside, and I sit down next to them. It makes me feel young. And then I deal with it all: methodically, almost mindlessly sometimes, one by one until there aren't any left. Most days it's all Trace Italian, but some days there'll be stragglers: maybe the Pennsylvania kids who answered an ad in a yellowing magazine they'd found at the Goodwill just to see what would happen, and who now competed against each other in an otherwise wholly abandoned game called Rise of the Sorcerers. War game fiends playing through Operation Mercury for the third or fourth time. Or one of the seven people who still play Scorpion Widow, who may well keep playing forever somehow, no matter what happens to me. Two today. Sometimes I let my mind drift out a little: I try not to get carried away, and I have to be careful, but I wonder about them, the servants of the scorpion widow— who they really are, what they're like. If they contemplate growing old along with their subscriptions. Maybe they'll go missing one day, stuck forever in the sands where they made their last move. Gone. Who might they be elsewhere: in their rooms, alone with pencils, working on maps. Why they play, why they're still here. What it means to them.

I sit there reading, and reading, and reading. I take the cash or checks they send and tuck them away into a money pouch I'll take down to the bank once a month. Some players write long letters that narrate their next move in great detail, explaining why they're doing one thing and not another, guessing at the perils of going the wrong way; others are just a sentence, or a fragment of one. *Leave silo and scope out street. Head for hills. Interrogate the traitor.*

Decrypting the letters is like detective work, but it's also like surgery: there's a lot of connective tissue, and some of it's wet and messy. People get invested in the game. They scatter details of their daily lives throughout their narratives; some friend who used to play the game but is gone now, God knows where—dead? lost? got too old?—will appear mid-letter, a ghost whispering an idea to the player as he writes. *If Jeff were playing, he'd probably attack the guard, but I'm not Jeff, so I'm going to wait until the guard falls asleep and remove the grating in the floor of the cell.* Things like that. Who's Jeff? Did I know him? I extract the necessary information from the greater narrative, and I pull the corresponding next move from the filing cabinet.

Every move I send out begins with the same word: *You.* When I first wrote most of them, so long ago now that it's incredible to think of it, I had in my mind only a single player, and of course he looked almost exactly like me: not me as I am now, but as I was before the accident. Young and fresh and frightened, and in need of refuge from the world. I was building myself a home on an imaginary planet. I hadn't considered, then, how big the world was; how many people lived there, how different their lives were from mine. The infinite number of planets spinning in space. I have since traveled great distances, and my sense of the vast oceans of people down here on the Earth, how they drift, is keener. But *you*, back then, was a singular noun for me, or, at best, a theoretical plural awaiting proof.

I went through my plural *you*s now. I sent one guy off to find a brass bowl for the eventual gathering of venom from the jaw of the scorpion widow herself, and I let another sweat through a long night on the beach at Crete, waiting for Nazis. I was taking my time about it, and I knew why, even though in my head I'd told myself: I'll just go back to my life as it was, back to the land of spectral effects. Nothing is really different now.

I have a deep need for stasis and for the most part I've gained it, over time. Even after the recent assaults my shield zone remained fairly strong. So I wanted to be telling myself the truth about where, in the state of play, I stood this morning. But I'd recognized a postmark going through the pile, and I'd set that one aside, knowing what it was going to be about. I try not to be dramatic about my life, no matter what turns it takes. There's nothing down that road for me. But I took a little breath, worming the tip of my index finger in under the seal and then ripping the envelope open down the side.

Hey Focus dude. Hope everything's cool with you. I'm just going to keep playing if that's OK. Maybe that seems weird to you I don't know. After all the stuff. It's not your fault you know, it isn't anybody's fault. There was other stuff going on with us not just the game. It's a whole thing you couldn't even know about. I am glad the judge dropped the lawsuit it was bullshit anyway. OK so I pick up the shovel by the disposal unit and start digging, all right? When we dug back in Tularosa it worked out all right. Anyway let me know what I find I am pretty sure there will be some antidote there. Love, Lance

It doesn't have anything to do with me, I thought. Just out on the edges, maybe. I am in a unique position to understand that. But back down where the old me lived, somewhere near the brain stem where everything gets basic, I could see how Lance would want to just forge forward. It seemed less crazy to me than it would have seemed to his parents. I picked out the "Dig Near Unit" move from the filing cabinet and I stuffed and sealed the envelope. I wrote *getting close!* over the seal. And I noticed that the envelope would be going to Lance in care of somebody else—a neighbor? a friend from school? I didn't know; I didn't need to know. I let the moment sort of evaporate as I slid the stuffed envelope into the tray marked *outgoing*. And I thought, you know, maybe tomorrow I will go to the park, or if not tomorrow, next week. I should go to the park, just to sit in the park and look at the world. I am working too hard, not that I mind. But I need to get out more. I'll go to the park and just sit, and see what comes up.

4 It was Teague I thought of when I first drew up the Tularosa fortune shack, and it was his face I saw when I dreamed up the astrologer inside it. I knew Teague from junior high. We'd gone to different elementary schools, but everybody in town got dumped into the same junior high. It was a scary place. Some of the kids from the other schools were bigger, meaner; you had to spend a lot of energy trying to avoid them. Teague was kind of short. His shoulders were starting to broaden, but he wore his hair long, and it opened him up to a lot of grief. Kids threw food at him when he walked through the cafeteria. He never even looked back at them.

We had Composition I together but Teague sat by himself, his head hanging low. Everybody called him Tits; they'd say it a bunch of times to try to make him look up. He'd be sitting there, eyes down, head tucked, pencil working, worlds away, when the hissing would start up. Just this through-the-teeth whispering chant, almost empty of meaning: not *Teague, you suck*, or *Teague, fuck you*, or anything. Just *Tits* over and over. During tests it sounded like a forest at night in the classroom.

Voices rising singly or several at a time from the focused quiet. *Tits. Tits. Titssss.*

I didn't call Teague *Tits*, because I wasn't any more popular than he was: I was just better at staying invisible. Sometimes he and I sat together on the metal tables over by the date palm in a corner of the lunch yard. He collected these hand-cast metal figurines of characters from *The Lord of the Rings* and he'd show them to me if I asked. I'd find him sitting there combing intensely through a stack of magazines with his right hand while holding a neglected sandwich in his left. He always looked like a guy who wanted to be left alone, but we'd talked about movies a couple of times in class and I felt like we were on the same side. I'd leave a little distance between us when I sat down just in case I was reading him wrong.

One day I was working on a slab of beef jerky and leafing through a book while I ate; it was Fritz Lieber's *Swords Against Death*. After a while, I noticed Teague peering over at me. He'd stopped looking at his magazines; all his attention was on me. It was like he was looking at a bug that'd been flipped over onto its back.

"What," I said when I noticed him.

"What's that book?" he said.

"*Swords Against Death*," I said.

He looked down at the cover, which had a boat on it and a monster with a trident rising out of the ocean. "Is it supposed to spell *sad*?" he said after a while.

"Is it . . . what?" I said.

"*Sad*," he said. "*Swords Against Death*." He tapped his index finger on my book, three times, harder than he needed to. "Look down the left side, that spells *SAD*."

"I don't think that's on purpose," I said.

"It's probably on purpose," he said. "They put a lot of things onto the covers of books and stuff." I didn't know what to say to that; Teague, with his figurines and his bound notebooks bulging with sketches of imaginary mountain ranges or mysteriously numbered dodecahedrons, their lines meticulous, was someone whose opinion I valued. He wasn't a big talker. When he spoke it carried weight.

So I didn't say anything. I went back to reading, and at some point Teague just wandered off toward the water fountains. The mood was different after he left. Nothing I could point to directly, just a feeling in the air, in the movement of the wind in the palm. Dark, primitive magic. Swords Against Death.

I could pace the perimeter of the backyard if I wanted, but you feel stupid walking around a fenced yard in the middle of the day. The dermatologist's wasn't too far from the house, and I knew the way; Mom drove me there twice a week. Everybody was still avoiding arguments, so when I said I wanted to walk to my appointment, Mom said, "OK," and Dad said, "You sure?" with his eyebrows raised gently. For a minute it felt almost like a normal family scene.

It was a Saturday morning; traffic was light. Just a block past the unmarked boundary between Pomona and Montclair was a place I'd been half noticing all my life, a house; there were plain houses on either side, but somebody ran a business out of this one. It stuck out. I remember seeing it from the car as a kid: this big red glowing plastic hand in the bay window, a banner reading PALMISTRY spannning the entire second-floor balcony rail. There was also a sandwich board halfway up the front walk, impossible to miss if you went by on foot. I knew its top line by heart. It said *A MAP OF THE FUTURE?* in rounded black letters. But you couldn't read the smaller text underneath from the street; most of it was written in cursive, painted directly onto the board. I had been curious about it forever.

Today the banner was down, and the sandwich board had been moved up to the porch. The door to the house was open; there was a moving truck in the driveway. There had to be some people around, but I didn't see any. Soon this place will be gone; who knows what will take its place. I thought how I'd walked past it innumerable times, wondering what it was like inside, and figured this was my last chance. So I climbed as casually as I could up the stairs to the porch, and then I'd breached the boundary, like entering a dream.

Close up I could read the rest of the board; what it actually said beneath the splash, in black letters on white primer bearing traces of visible effort, was *Science of palmistry reaches back over three thousand years.* That was the top line. It was followed by a dozen others, evenly spaced, nearly uniform, each headed by a small, hand-painted tricolor image of Saturn. *Identify spiritual patterns using ancient techniques* was one. *Secrets of the Seven Minor Lines* was another. *Reunite a lost love.* The big door, beveled glass in oak, had to be at least fifty years old, maybe eighty. Old California stuff. Its decorated oval brass handle was half-black from wear.

What happens if I go inside? I wondered; it felt like a speech bubble forming over my head. Are all the people already gone?

I thought I might sneak in and steal something cool, maybe disappear before anybody knew I'd been there; I fantasized for a minute about making off with some small, secret object infused with magic power. I try to be careful about the things I think, but I was still young then, and in my rapidly forming dream scenario I could feel the mystery object in my hand, hot and dense. I was sweeping it from a glass end table in one smooth gesture. It had a deep, dark hue and hard hexagonal edges. When my vision cleared, I looked up to see some guy in painter's pants coming down a staircase inside, carrying a cardboard box.

He was probably a mover, but he could have been one of the people who lived there. Maybe the palmist himself, who knows. But he walked down the side of the porch right past me, undistracted by my glistening folds and reconstructed arches, too busy to notice. He looked back at me and smiled once he'd loaded the box onto the truck. "None today, friend," he said in a very neutral voice; he sounded calm and kind, but I felt afraid of him, as if some threat were implied in the deep recesses of the moment. So I went back down the steps and out to the street, imaginary eyes following my path as I went. I was still getting used to the feeling of being watched. I hated it.

Sometimes I can't remember whether this empty exchange happened before the accident or after, even though the details as I remember them point toward "after": the dermatologist, the place closing, the moving truck. If, for a few seconds, I entertain the idea that this scene takes place much earlier than it actually must have, something happens to me: I picture myself young and free, whole, getting gently warned off the property by the palmist or the palmist's husband for no real reason. And then some secret forms in a distant nebula somewhere, and somehow I get news of it, and I close my eyes and fall weightless through inner space for as long as I can stand it.

I dropped the astrologer shack into the middle of the New Mexico desert; I got the idea for it that day at the dermatologist's office, going through old issues of *National Geographic*. There was a big spread about the Tularosa Basin. The pictures called out from the pages: white sands with miraculous green growth jutting up in patches, skies whose pretty clouds held some empty menace that the lens couldn't translate fully. The Tularosa Basin was where they'd tested the atomic bomb before dropping it on Japan. I sat waiting for the secretary to call my name, gazing into these pictures of the basin, how it looked years later. When I got home that day, I took out the Trace Italian master map and sketched a little line drawing of a hut no bigger than my fingernail, and around it I drew a loose oval, its line quivering with cilia and sudden jagged outcroppings. In small capital letters I wrote TULAROSA FORTUNE SHACK HERE.

I saw Teague at the Book Exchange last week. It's twenty years on now, but there we were, still both haunting the science fiction section, running our index fingers down the fraying spines. His hair's shorter now but he looked more like his younger self than a lot of other people might after so much time.

He started talking like he was picking up a thread I'd just set down a minute ago. "Hey, man," he said. "I just want to say I meant to stop back by after the first time but I didn't think your folks were too into it. I sent some books with Kimmy but they might have gotten intercepted."

"Teague!" I said.

"Yeah, man," he said. "I was gonna come some more but your dad, you know."

"I don't even remember ever seeing you after my last day at school," I said.

"I guess not," he said. "I was there on, like, the second day. You were in the ICU. They had you on a lot of drugs. You called me Marco. Your dad thought it was some kind of code."

It was like talking to a character in an old movie, hearing lines read out from some earlier, remembered time.

"Out in the hallway he told me just not to come back. I wasn't really in a place where I could fight with your dad, and he was out there pacing around in front of your door like he was itching for an excuse to go off on somebody. And, like . . . didn't you guys used to go on hunting trips?"

"Yeah, yeah," I said.

"Jesus Christ, man," he said. I wished I'd kept in touch with Teague. We could have talked. But the path from there to here consisted of infinite switchbacks in countless interlocking chains. The trail broke off from the main road almost the second the shot rang out.

"I knew your mom OK, and I thought I could probably finesse things if I tried, but—I just didn't, is all. I didn't really think you were going to make it," he said, as blunt as when he was young, an old friend.

"I did, though." It was good to see Teague, still in the world.

"Oh, I know," he said, flipping a copy of *The Dreaming*

Jewels out from the shelf. "I played one of your games through once. Teague's just a nickname, you know."

"Wait, really?" This was news.

"Yeah," he said. "*Tigger*. From the Winnie-the-Pooh books. From when I was a kid."

I played one of your games through once. I wanted to ask, but there was something special in not knowing.

"Anyway, sorry I never said anything. I guess I figured since you never let on you knew me maybe you just didn't want to talk."

"It was pretty hard to talk to me then," I said.

"Aww, man," he said. "Are you OK, though? I saw some news story."

"Recently?"

"Yeah, yeah. Recently."

I'd been wondering; now I knew. "Yeah," I said. "It looked bad but it's OK now, I guess. Blew over after a while. Just in the past couple of days. Still getting my head around it."

As we spoke I kept digging around in my mind trying to place his last name, but Teague was just Teague. I wouldn't have heard his last name since roll call in some unremembered class over twenty years ago.

"Keith Jones," I said when it came to me.

"Man, don't call me that, nobody calls me that," he said. We wrote each other's numbers down, but in my heart I knew this was it.

Inside the shack the first thing you learn is that the astrologer is dead. *You see the body of a man in a strange costume* is how

39

the turn begins: *He is lying on the floor, his face twisted into a grimace.* Smart players will spend the next turn searching for protective clothing and masks; overeager players will get sick when they leave this scene, and they'll stay sick for a while. The air inside the shack is unbreathably thick with the smell of blood and candle wax and lamp oil and empty insect bodies. Charts and notebooks lie open around the corpse in a constellation; if you marked its points and drew a line connecting them, you'd have a shape that would later help open a door deep within the Trace, but nobody will ever notice this, or learn the name of the door, which you have to say when you open it or you end up in a blind corridor that traps you for at least four turns, which would probably outrage any players who made it that far. But who knows. What it would be like to make it that far is sheer conjecture.

Players who've got their protective gear on are free to look around and loot the place, but of course the whole point is the charts. You have to read them, and then you have to remember what you've read, or keep your game organized enough to go back and consult them later. You should, anyway; that's the good they can do. But even if you just read through your turn passively, READ CHARTS tries to pay you back for your effort. *HOUSE OF SCORPIO SCORPIO HOUSE STONE SARDONIX COLOR GOLD*, it starts. *IF SCORPIO ENTERING SOUTH DOOR HIGH LIGHT ALL OTHER DOORS WEST LIGHT, ALL OTHER SCORPIO DOORS WEST LIGHT WEST.* I feel my own freedom remembering this turn, what it means to find a place where the world's shut out for good at last, where all signs point back at one another and the overall pattern's clear if you look hard enough. *HOUSE OF NEPTUNE MARSH BEAST, RIVER BEAST, CLOUD-COVER GOOD, DRY*

COVER AVOID/AVOID. HOUSE OF LIBRA FISH NAME SECRET, SAY W/ EYE CONTACT AT ALL DOORS IN HOUSE OF LIBRA, ALL AD-MITTANCE GAIN, ALL DOORS. HOUSE OF GEMINI GEMINI HOUSE STONE CHRYSOPRASE COLOR GREEN, the chambers in the Trace outnumbering stars in the sky and all the sands on all the beaches: IF GEMINI ENTERING FROM NORTH BEAR ORCHID, MY RESEARCH INDICATES and then three lines about various kinds of orchids and where they're from, cribbed from who knows where and saved here, forever. There are twelve charts in all; it's one of the longest turns in the game, and I probably over-did it a little, but every time I have to triple-crease the several sheets that make up the move, I smile.

If you go north after escaping Las Vegas you can skip the astrologer shack. The jagged route east will take you to a state fairgrounds; there's lots to do there. But most people look at the straight line on the map and follow it like a beacon, and then they get their fortunes told. I've had people get a little angry about the sequence once or twice, people who after receiving "You Have Arrived At The Small Shack of a Local Astrologer" feel like they deserve a little more action for their money. But when they get inside the shack their tone shifts. There's power in thinking you're about to meet somebody who knows what's next for you, and there's another level of power in seeing that person's body on the floor, having to get the information from him somehow now that he's no longer in any condition to give it. This latter power is the greater power, full of dark, worldly secrets that you have to go out of your way to find out about, and I consider it something to be avoided, but I force everybody's hand all the same; if you want to avoid the astrologer you have to put in extra work. Some do manage to shrug off my cues and go around, or go past without looking, or even get so far as approaching the door but get scared off instead of intrigued by the smell. I can see how they'd think they were being warned instead of lured, but the ones who don't go in are in some way strangers to me.

Most players just drift off eventually. Their focus wanders; their interests shift. Maybe they finish their games stealthily, like Teague had, like who-knows-who-else had over the years. Chris Haynes was different. He'd been different in his gameplay from the day of his first move; his letters appeared as the fruit of long, careful consideration, small, smooth, dense bursts of thought in flowing script, punctuation adhering to some internal rhythm that was easy to pick up on and easy to follow, grammar not quite holding together but always moving the play forward. *"Sean, everybody says that's your name so OK,"* one started.

> *I've been in Lordsburg for two turns, total ghost town now, time for me to re-hit the path. If the active ingredients in the roots of the flowers around here haven't been weakened by radiation exposure, which technically I don't think they should have been because (A) the river, and (B) they're flowering normally, I refer you to the text of three turns back, "a few flowers poke up near the bank of the river," not big flowers or spectacular flowers just flowers, then my health should be back to 85% because I have been eating every root I see. Even better, flowering root plants mean it's April? Late March, latest? So I can*

head north. I'm going to head north. As of last turn
my choice was between a companion from an occupied
schoolyard (no) or trying to wrangle a golf cart. I'm
going golf cart. Let me know how it plays out

and then his initials, a cipher, something I could imagine him working out in grade school and holding on to all his life. *CH.* Write it again until every one's exactly the same. Get so you can carve it into a desktop with a paper clip in one class period. A *C* whose high line arced but whose bottom line was straight, nearly the outline of a human eye but with a gap at the right, and then that tiny *H* inside it like an alien pupil. *CH.* Several times a month. *CH.*

I wonder if I'd remember Chris as fondly as I do if he hadn't quit the game, but he did quit, formally, which as I say is not usually how it happens. Usually, people just seem to drift in their attention; long gaps form between their turns, and then at some point they don't renew their subscriptions and I stop hearing from them. "Growing out of it" is the phrase that comes to mind, but this is an obviously problematic view for me, so I try not to analyze it much further than the bare facts. Something happens over time, and people stop playing. General rule. Except for Chris, who let me know why.

I got up last night at 2 am thinking about how to repair my rifle, I don't even have a rifle except in the Trace, his final move began.

I was asleep, then I was awake, and the first thing I
thought about when I woke up was this rifle with the
special attachment I took from the fortune-teller's body, a

body I took three turns to find and another turn to strip
of anything useful to me and Sean I could smell body
when I thought about this, hot New Mexico sun human
body and so I don't think I can play anymore. It's not like
I think anything's going to happen, I'm fine, and I don't
actually have anything better to do, and it doesn't take
up too TOO much of my time? But it's in my head now
and I don't want it anymore so I'm going free-play here,
<u>you have to let me do this</u>.

If you are a person whose authority is generally limited to his own small life and to a series of imaginary choices that exist on a vast but comprehensible grid, it's odd when you hear someone, across the impersonal distance of the page, pleading for your permission. I thought of this during the preparation for the trial, when I was leafing through my files and arguing with myself about burning things, or maybe ripping them to pieces and driving them out to a dumpster in a parking lot somewhere. But all that was too much drama, too much action, too much of everything: setting things on fire, heading off somewhere to hide the proof that they'd once existed. I had spent too long clearing a path that told its own story, and it was a straight path. That was its whole appeal. The path to the Trace is different from other paths; that difference is supposed to make up for something.

This new turn from you tells me what all I got by
cleaning out the corpse of the fortune-teller. OK. I got
silver earrings and some crystals and some old money

and some vials of something that I bet are anti-infective stuff, and I got a knife with crescent moon in the handle of it. OK. I am saying that the knife is a pretty big knife that my dude has been using to skin deer. I drag his body out behind his shack and I use the knife to dig in the dirt behind the house. The dirt is a little soft because it's near the house getting some shadow instead of out under the baking sun all day. I get tired but I clear just enough space to get this guy in. I don't know who killed him and nobody's ever going to know. I scoop enough dirt back on top of him to cover his body and I say out loud something about how I hope all seekers make it to where they're going and then I take the knife and stab myself in the neck. I bleed out on top of the fortune-teller's grave and then I'm dead and that's my game. I am OK and I'll be OK but this is the end and this is my story. CH.

I remember reading that turn through at my desk, the ancient, heavy wooden desk I'd gotten for thirty dollars at Goodwill, half-stripped of a deep red paint that was never going to give itself up entirely, dozens of interlocking grooves left across its top by countless ballpoint pens pushed down too hard onto unblotted paper. I remember feeling with total confidence that everything was all right with Chris, that he had made the right move. I took a piece of 8½ × 11 paper from a drawer and found an old charcoal pencil with a nice thick nub and I made out his death certificate. *Chris Haynes pronounced dead this day by own hand b. (   ) d. Tularosa. I do hereby affirm the truth of this document by affixing my signature hereto,*

45

here followed by an intentionally illegible signature, *county coroner, Trace Italian Kansas.* It looked ragged and blunt, appropriately Old West. My signature bore no resemblance to my actual signature in the real world; I did it with my left hand. I take a lot of pride in my work.

5 When I got back from the courthouse I was pretty shaken up. The only thing I really felt like doing was lying down on the floor in the den with the television on and all the lights off. First I tried a little plain old broadcast TV: some news, and a few minutes of a cooking show, and an old episode of *Family Ties*. But I couldn't focus. I was agitated; the strategies I'd developed for shutting down the several tape loops running concurrently in my head weren't working.

The judge had dismissed the case against me without prejudice, saying he couldn't reasonably imagine another judge looking at the same evidence and coming to a different conclusion, etcetera, but that he wanted to leave a door open in the interest of justice being served in the event of new evidence coming to light, and so on. But his tone, and his gentle manner, conveyed his true meaning to everybody in the room; he didn't want to seem heartless, so he'd tried softening the blow. But he'd been telegraphing his punches from fairly early on: in the questions he directed to Carrie's parents. In the silences that grew between their responses and his subsequent remarks. Even his bearing while seated, those deep-rising heavy black-robed breaths, seemed to be preparing everyone to hear his opinion.

That opinion, which carried legal force, was that there was no case here. No reason to go forward. Just several sad people and their partially wrecked lives. Once he'd spoken I was technically out of the woods. But my head: my head was all messed up. In video games you sometimes run into what they call a side quest, and if you don't manage to figure it out you can usually just go back into the normal world of the game and continue on toward your objective. I felt like I couldn't find my way back to the world now: like I was somebody locked in a meaningless side quest, in a stuck screen.

So I went to the kitchen and I made myself a sandwich, and I cut it up into manageable pieces so I could eat with a fork. And then I drove down to Cinema Video. I can hardly believe Cinema Video's still in business, and I really can't believe how many videotapes they still have in there, gathering dust against the east wall. But look down toward your feet and they're all right there, neatly piled up in hopeful stacks on the floor. There's a little sign taped to the wall at about knee level, green marker on canary-colored copier paper: *Used Tapes $5.00*.

Stacks of dusty VHS tapes automatically register to the eye as trash now, and I'd be surprised if anybody ever took much note of the sign or the hoard it pointed toward. But I got out a twenty and I brought home four: *Future-Kill*, *Krull*, *Red Sonja*, and *Gor*. It was a little bracing to carry *Gor* up to the counter, because when I was a kid I used to think about *Gor* the way some kids thought about making the football squad. It was an object of almost religious contemplation. I would scrutinize John Norman paperbacks in the Thrifty book rack like a code cracker working against the clock.

There were so many *Gor* books. No end to them. *Marauders of Gor. Slave Girl of Gor. Priest Kings of Gor.* They stared out from the same shelf as Doc Savage at the Book Exchange, but Doc Savage books were different, because you could tell the publishers wanted you to like them. Afternoons had been spent in meetings and at drawing boards coming up with the right combinations of images and cover copy, and by the time the books reached the racks, they were rich with code: images for the curious, images for the devout, all threaded together. They faced the world with action scenes promising adventure and intrigue, and the promise of triumph over fantastic adversity or final glory at its hands. Who doesn't want to rise above the obstacles in his pathway? Who wouldn't want to go down in flames? And for those of us who can't or won't rise above, who doesn't at least want to hear stories about how it might be possible for some triumph to eventually happen, given enough luck?

The *Gor* books, by contrast, were shameful and garish. The pictures on their covers were pornographic, but in an almost dishonest way: near-nude mutants leering out into the fluorescent air of the drugstore aisle. Willingly or not, they seemed to suggest that maybe you shouldn't actually be reading these books. And so I never did. I would stare at their covers, and maybe thumb through them a little, picking out phrases and images like a secret shoplifter. But that would be enough for me, and sometimes more than enough. I didn't need to hear the stories the books were trying to sell me: their skins haunted and troubled me enough. But I would assemble my own stories, based on the information I had from the covers; and in my stories, there'd be winners, victors, spoils to divide, satisfying conclusions to things. Happy endings sometimes. I felt sure that the books themselves would be less kind to their characters, that whatever was actually going on inside was dark and mirthless. There was this odd, flat sort of desolation in those covers. Steam or smoke rising from a distant city, seen from a boat out on the water: grimy, vivid. It always made me feel uneasy.

I set the stack of movies down in front of the TV when I got back, and I pulled the VCR out of the closet and wired everything together. I thought about *Gor*, but it still had some sort of prohibitive power over me, so I turned out the lights and sat in my recliner watching *Krull*. It took me back. The screen throbbed in its familiar way and the darkness around it spread out to the farthest corners of the room. When the movie was over I just sat there in my chair for a while. The sun was going down outside. I nodded off and caught one of those ten-minute naps that always feel like they last longer than they really do.

I dreamed of a ghost in a hallway; the ghost was holding his own head in his hands. I know where this image came from, and I knew in the dream, too, though that didn't make it less real or frightening. The ghost holding his own head in his hands, coming down a hallway, was a neither-common-nor-rare card in the Monsters of the World series. These were bubble gum cards with a stiff stale powdery pink slab of gum included in every pack; I used to buy them at Rexall. Kids would joke about buying the cards and throwing the gum away, but nobody actually threw the gum away, because they had paid for it. It crunched when you chewed it.

Some people dream whole stories, but I get only fleeting images. A ghost in a hallway, an open hallway facing out onto some trees. Maybe an office building in California. Maybe an apartment complex. The ghost is holding his head in his hands, making a ghost sound. I'm not even sure how I know it's a ghost; his flesh is solid. The face is held close against the ghost's body, so from where I'm standing, I can see only the back of his head.

Sometimes I try to make my dreams mean something: to connect them to the accident, which seems like an obvious fit here, or to connect them to things going on in my life. But there's so little to them, so little to pick apart in my dreams. A thing that's a ghost because something tells me that's what it is, coming toward me in a hallway of some building. No real details. Ghost, hallway, building. When I woke up, I thought about Kansas, cold Kansas where the hallways of the buildings would be tightly sealed against the weather, so unlike the open, exposed buildings of Southern California, which are the only buildings I can actually tell you anything about, because they're the only ones I've ever seen with my own eyes.

Krull is a movie about a man on a quest, and it plays like something made by guileless people. Who knows the secrets of anybody's heart, I guess: for all I know everyone involved with *Krull* has bodies under the floorboards and babies in the oven. But the evidence on the screen strongly suggests that these were people trying to make something fun for others to enjoy, something largely innocent, not trying to open up any windows on the abyss. For me, though, it was a hallway full of doors leading to dark places. The hearing at the courthouse had propped several of these doors ajar: bagged bits of evidence standing in for bigger questions that couldn't be answered, timelines of meaningless afternoons that ended somewhere big and terrible. But whether they'd seen it coming or not, the abyss had eventually gotten around to claiming most of the people who made the movie, or starred in it, or underwrote its considerable budget. The abyss was general. Which I couldn't help thinking, the whole time: I was twelve when I first saw ads for this movie running in the *L.A. Times*. How old does that make some of those young people on my screen now? Who's left?

The plotline was fairly clear. *This was given to me to know: that many worlds have been enslaved by the beast and his army the slayers.* It aimed high; I could feel the old excited hopes, destined for disappointment but still game, rising up inside me. Everything came together: the potential letdown of the saccharine wedding at the outset suddenly ripped into vivid pieces by the electric-blue flashing doors and the slayers scaling the walls. Swords that gave off lightning when they clashed, full-screen flaring X's in battles whose backstories hadn't been filled in sufficiently yet, so that the central remaining image for me—then as now—was the crystal-clean desolation of the aftermath: Confusion. Sudden loss. Evaporating bodies in an emptied stone cathedral. One guy looked like somebody I used to hang out with, I thought, watching his face turn to steam. Was it JJ? Maybe. I couldn't even get a clear picture of JJ in my mind anymore. It had been too long.

I drifted off into the sanctity of my earliest, angrier visions of the Trace Italian as the screen dimmed and flashed. A band of thieves led by the newly crowned king heading through mountains that looked identical to the ones a few miles north of my house. The quest to recover the kidnapped queen from the clutches of the beast. Distractions that killed people: kindly old wizards possessed by things that turned their eyes black and left their bodies empty shriveled husks atop the swamp. Calm marshlands from whose mists steel-clad killers rose suddenly, their muffled electronic screams grabbing hold of something inside me that was basic, primal, essential. The nearing of the goal. Dark caves. Lava streams that reminded me, and only me—but what was the difference—of the little fountain that used to flow at the center of Montclair Plaza. The battle of the king against the beast for his kingdom and its spoils. The worm left in the king's brain, and in mine, by the few things the beast says before going down howling, felled by a magical throwing star that only the king could wield.

What the movie was really about was ambition, and what a fine thing it could come to seem, given the right light. It was about coming of age, and the rich reward waiting for those who went through it with courage. The brave and true of heart prevailed, and the usurpers got their due. One world escaped the slavemaster's grasp. The wicked went down to perdition and the good folk prospered.

It was too high-minded to satisfy my seething adolescent brain, whose permanent thirst for blood I'd been hoping to feed, I now realized. And I wondered why I'd want to feed a monster I'd spent much of my adult life trying to bury; but I set that question off to one side. Because the story wasn't the point, wasn't what was troubling me. It was the little details, the stage on which it was set, the margins. The trappings of the greater story—the props, the scenery, the special effects—those were what held me, what spoke to me. In them I recognized the guessed-at originals of my crude early visions, the ones that would grow over time. The caves, the castle, the final battleground: these were all signposts on the road to the Trace.

But the Trace that Lance and Carrie'd found did not teem with lush growth or offer breathtaking vistas. There were no swamps to pass through en route to it, and it had not terminated in any final confrontation with some immense evil made flesh, towering arrogant and glowing in the sky above them. There had been at Lance and Carrie's sides no parties of fellow travelers, noble thieves, or inevitable tragic figures, joined together in common or disparate cause toward one victorious end. The terminus of their dreams, whose architecture may or may not have originated in me, had been a burrowing into dead earth. Its conclusion was neither climax nor punch line; it wasn't even a conclusion at all, except for Carrie. It was a headline in *The Wichita Eagle. One Dead, One Critical in Sci-Fi Game Pact.* The young king with his eyes toward the open mouth of the serpent, its voice cavernous: *You have chosen a paltry kingdom on an insignificant planet.*

6 The worst part of the hearing was I guess the presentation of the various artifacts, the unboxing of the bits and pieces that the prosecution had rounded up preparing for trial. Testimonials and letters, various receipts. Rough ideas in fabric. These were blueprints for a case no one would ever end up making, and their imagined barbs would go no further than the fat folders in which they'd been collated; they did find a home in me, though, and lodged there, like particles in a bedridden patient's lungs.

There was for example a postcard bought at the Flying J, a point of origin determined from receipts found in the abandoned car. It had been written at a Qdoba, though, from whose window one could see the highway, and it had then been addressed to me; they knew this because the text on the postcard said so, and also because detectives had visited the Qdoba in question in the course of their investigation, where they'd asked the manager whether he remembered some teenagers stopping through and writing a postcard either before or after or during their lunch. Naturally the manager of the Qdoba didn't remember any particular teenagers who'd had lunch there, but he did volunteer to ask his employees whether any of them remembered anything. One of them, eventually, did remember something, or thought he did, and so the claims the postcard made for itself were allowed to be discussed without anybody arguing about it.

It was numbing, but only down to a certain level, past which there can be no numbness. Lance and Carrie had written: *Got this postcard at a flying j but we're at qdoba now. next time you hear from us we will be inside!!* There was no need to reassemble the circumstances of the postcard's purchase, its meaningless life on its way to me; it did that by itself. All that was left for me to do with it was hold it in my hands and answer a question or two: yes, the business to which this postcard is addressed is Focus Games; yes, I do business under that name; yes, I notice that there's no stamp on the card; no, I couldn't guess why it wasn't stamped and sent (I wanted to guess, because I had some guesses, but my attorney had advised me against trying any of my guesses out loud). No, as I had told them all before, I had never been to Kansas. No, I did not know why Qdoba. No, I had never eaten at such a place, or mentioned it in passing in any of my correspondences with customers. Yes, I understood why they were asking me about the Qdoba. They were asking me because it was the last place anybody had ever seen Carrie alive.

Carrie's parents had flown in from Orlando. They'd been staying in a motel by the freeway for weeks. It was a safe bet that their lawyer would have warned them by then about what to expect from my physical appearance, but unless you work in the medical field somewhere, you can't really be prepared to meet me, I don't think. It is always a surprise. It's just not a thought people can get their teeth around, having to brace themselves to meet someone at whom it will be difficult to look while he's talking but whose speech they will strain to understand.

They were brave. My lawyer and I entered the room; she nodded her hellos to the prosecutor and the judge while I kept my head low like I always do, and then we took our seats on our side of the table. Carrie's parents—Dave and Anna; Anna and Dave: I could never decide how to pair them in my mind—fixed me with a look that I imagine had taken some practice, but which was sincere. There was not a whole lot of anger left in it, though traces lingered here and there: in the crow's-feet by their eyes and the bags under them, say. In the way their eyebrows didn't rise when they nodded. But the main thing their expressions indicated was a sense of duty. It pained me to think about it.

The judge read out a few things about the nature of pretrial hearings and about what we were here to do, and then things opened up a little: it was like a refereed argument between people who weren't allowed to address each other directly. Their lawyer stated what their case essentially amounted to—that I'd contributed to the endangerment of a minor both directly and indirectly, and that this had resulted in the death of one and the grave injury of another: manslaughter and attempted manslaughter—and mine tried politely to say that you'd have to be crazy to blame anybody besides Lance and Carrie for what they'd done.

I focused on my breathing, because I knew my lawyer was

eventually going to read my statement, and I wanted her to get it over with; I'd hoped it would come out right at the beginning, so that Dave and Anna could either accept it forgivingly or reject it scornfully, and then I'd at least know where I stood. Until they'd heard what I had to say, I figured, there wasn't really any way of seeing their hand. It was impossible for me to imagine any scenario other than those two: total understanding or total denial. Either they'd get what I meant, or they'd shut their ears to it and we'd head down our sad road together. I didn't see a third way.

Where the railroad used to run, there's a little less overgrowth. As you travel, you keep your eyes on the ground ahead of you, trying to make out a path. Hours turn into days. You become a human bloodhound. You notice things others didn't as they tried and failed to walk the path that now is yours. As you progress the path becomes less clear: with every less clear point you know you're going beyond the places where the others lost the trail. Stopping to rest, you see a spot where plants seem to grow higher. If they have followed your path faithfully, bounty hunters will be here within the hour. North lies Nebraska.

This turn came accompanied by one of my occasional bonuses, a status upgrade. It was an aluminum coin; I'd had fifty of them minted for me by one of the companies that made tokens for video games, back when there'd been a video arcade in every mall. There was a picture of a dome rising from an empty plain on one side, and on the other, it said PATHFINDER. I had only ever had to send out three of these coins over the years. Two of them were in the hands of longtime players in distant places. The other was in a plastic bag labeled EVIDENCE on the table in front of me.

I felt embarrassed when the text of the turn was read out loud at the hearing; most of Trace Italian's latter turns were essentially first drafts, since hardly anyone ever saw them. They were turns in theory, not practice. Some were actually relics from all those long days in the hospital, formulae I'd memorized to keep myself from going insane during nights when I couldn't sleep because of the pain in my jaw, or from days when the ringing in my ears demanded that I focus very hard on something until the sound died down. None of them were anything I'd looked at in years until Lance and Carrie'd gotten to them; they were crude artifacts to me now, or like somebody else's work imitating mine. Given the whole thing to do over again, I might have written the late moves better, focused harder on the phrasing. But I hadn't, and now they were cast in stone. I'd thought once or twice about revisiting them, but I didn't have the stomach for it. Trace Italian had existed long enough to have earned self-determination. I didn't feel like I had the right to revise it. That right belonged to the younger man who'd written the game, and that younger man was dead. Besides, there were people playing toward the latter moves; the moves had to remain as they were in case anyone ever got there. It seemed almost a moral question.

Like all turns, this one ended with the player's options presented as an unnumbered list of possibilities in typewritten capital letters, each possible next move occupying its own line of type. When, in the hearing room, the turn was handed around the table for all to examine, I smiled a little inside. I had tried, so long ago, to limit the player's options if he ever came to this pass. I had failed, but the effort seemed clever.

```
FORAGE FOR ROOTS
FOLLOW THE RAILROAD
WAIT FOR HUNTERS
NORTH TO NEBRASKA
```

When I was a child, my mind wandered a lot, and most often it would wander to the dark places, as though drawn there by instinct. It found them again now. I saw Lance and Carrie freezing in the middle of the hard Kansas night. I imagined their hunger. I remembered skimming the autopsy report: Carrie died early; her coat was thinner. What had it been like for Lance, lying in the dark, waiting to be next? The pit they'd dug for themselves: Had it bought them some time? Or had the energy they'd wasted digging shortened the time they'd had left? Does a person gasp like a dying old man when he's dying of cold, or is it different? Did they see their nail beds going blue, and feel panic, or had their minds gone past the point of panic to that self-drugged state where everything looks cool? And why hadn't they gotten up and run back to the highway—no energy left? Still convinced they'd find something? Did both of them want to bolt from the scene but neither one want to blink first? Their young, perfect bodies, wasted, squandered, covered in the end with wet grass they'd pulled into the pit from the surrounding plain. Trying to put it off. Children. Children in the grip of a vision whose origins lay down within my own young dreams, in the wild freedom those dreams had represented for me, in my desperation: to build and destroy and rebuild, to create mazes on blank pages.

I let the evidence bag rest flat on my upturned palms, as if it were some historical document of great value or interest. I looked at it, remembered a whole bunch of things from my own distant past, and then recalled the day the turn had come back to me in the mail with none of the options circled. Instead, in pencil, a fifth way: a mystery at the time, a bad punch line now. Of all the things that made me wince, this was the one that hit me hardest, because there was hope in it: determination, drive, all that youthful focus. Two words, one compact phrase, handwritten in one script: one person signing for two. *START DIGGING. L+C.*

My lawyer read my statement.

> *I wish I could read this to you myself instead of having somebody read it for me. It's not like I can't talk, but it is distracting to other people when I do. So I have written it down. I hope you both can understand.*
>
> *It would be an insult to you and to the memory of your daughter for me to spend too much time dwelling on who I am and what I am like as a person. I imagine your attorneys have explained to you how I got to be the way I am. I have no children of my own. I can't imagine what you are going through.*
>
> *I spent most of my teenage years in hospitals and physical therapy rehabs. It gets so lonely living inside your own head. Because of my face I could not even wear*

headphones for listening to music. So I invented a world in the future and I called it the Trace Italian. It was a place where I could have adventures, and when I grew up, I wanted to share those adventures with other people. I wanted specifically to share them with people like me, but I don't know any people like me. Most people like me are dead.

I don't have close personal friends but my customers are like friends to me. I share in their lives a little. To them I am just a company, and that is fine. I live a little through them and the small things I learn about them. It makes my own life feel more interesting. I don't go to conventions to meet with them or personalize my business, and I don't answer personal mail; I don't want to be a creep. I am only here to provide a service. I have taken pride in that service, and my work has brought me pleasure over the years, and I never, ever thought anyone could possibly come to harm from it. If I had thought someone would get hurt because of Trace Italian, I would have shut it down. I would not even have started it in the first place. Lance and Carrie played the game together and did so well that I was amazed. I thought they were just two smart kids. Anybody would have predicted a great future for them both.

I understand that you blame me and I can't be angry about that but I ask you to look at things my way. However different I am from normal people, in the end I am just a guy trying to do his job. Trace Italian doesn't stand for anything in the real world and I couldn't have guessed anyone would ever think otherwise. I hardly know

*anything about the real world. What little I do know
I got from books and movies. I did not knowingly send
any young people to their deaths. I would not. I couldn't.
Please understand. It is a little strange to me, to be
defending something that was supposed to have been a
place where people could feel safe and have fun, where
nothing ever really happens except inside our heads. But
understand too that I have to defend myself and my
creation that has brought pleasure to a few people over
the years. The Trace is a good place. It is a place where
people can go, in their imaginations. That is a good
thing and while I'm sorry it went wrong for your
daughter it is not wrong by itself.*

*By the way and against advice of counsel I want to
say that Lance and Carrie were technically right. Of the
four possibilities on the paper, the one that would have
moved them in the direction they wanted to go was
FORAGE FOR ROOTS. I don't know why I want to tell you
this. I know it doesn't help my case. I just feel like I owe it
to them to let you know. They were right to start digging.
But they were only right to start digging in the game, not
out in the real world. Not in Kansas in actual ground.
I am so so sorry.*

I had to fight to keep my bearings, hearing it read out loud;
there's a gap between things I write down and what they'd
sound like if I were to try to say them. My grief sought out all
parts of my body it hadn't yet inhabited, and I felt like I might
collapse in on myself right there, at last, spectacularly. I'd left
out a lot of things I'd wanted to throw in: Chris Haynes, for

instance, how I felt like his exit proved there was nothing wrong with living in dreams as long as you didn't let yourself get carried away. But I had been advised—"in the strongest terms," they'd said, looking harder at me than most people ever dare, driving the point home as deeply as they could—to make no reference to other players, to anything anyone else had ever done inside the playfield. When I brought up Chris's name, they'd held up their hands, no-thank-you style: counter-examples might end up being part of my defense, they said; it was "protected," we could get to all that later if it went to trial. "Don't get defensive," they said. They meant *Don't get mad*. I tried, but I felt the impulse moving: as I wrote, as I listened. Don't these people know I'd never hurt anybody again? But I couldn't let myself think like that. Too much terrain off out there. So I wrote what I wrote, and the clear, level voice of my lawyer presented it to the sterile field of the conference room, and I sat there as still as a stone.

Nobody looked at anybody else for a second. It was like a scene from a dream. And then my lawyer rose and said, Your honor, Lance's parents aren't here because they don't believe my client bears any responsibility for their son's current condition. She paused for a second, and then she presented the signed affidavits: Lance's parents had written them and agreed to have them read at the hearing. Copies of the affidavits went around the table until everybody had one, and then we all followed along while the reporter read them into the record. The mood changed; Lance's parents lived in a world far from the room where we seven had gathered. Their days were spent with terms like *long-term care*, and in the eternal tangle of insurance forms. They said that Lance had always had problems;

they didn't think Lance's problems had been anybody's fault, and besides, he had new problems now. They were more interested in the future than in the past, no matter how hard the past had been. They were putting all that behind them.

There was silence for a minute, and then the judge, a little crudely I thought, nodded toward Dave and Anna, saying, "Well, this makes your case a lot harder to make, I think," and there were some concluding statements, but none of them really mattered. People rose to speak and sat back down again, but it was pretty obvious that none of it was going anywhere. You could feel something giving up in the air. Eventually the judge said he'd take a brief recess and come back with his decision, and we all went out into the hallway and milled around. My capacity for vanishing into whatever shadows happen to be around is a hard-won and precious skill. Then we reconvened in the side-room, and we listened while the judge read out his ruling, and that was the end of that. I didn't feel like I'd really won anything, but I had come through the day no worse off than I'd come into it, which, as I have been telling myself for many years now, is a victory whether it feels like one or not.

7 The supermarket is for me what the beach is for other people: it's eternal. I remember riding there in the car with my mom, once or twice a week every week; that out-of-time hour pushing the cart up and down the aisles, me wandering off to the magazine section when I got bored, always coming back with a copy of *Hit Parader* in hand. Or *Circus*. I liked *Hit Parader* better on principle because it printed song lyrics, but *Circus* had better stories and a much cooler name. I'd sneak copies into the basket and she'd feign surprise at seeing them when we got to the checkout. Our supermarket outings spanned the years from childhood to adolescence right up until the big change. It was a natural ritual: unscheduled, unchanging, traditional. *We're out of coffee, Sean, do you want to go to the supermarket? Yes. Yes, I do.*

So I have to say that I miss shopping. I miss it because it's something I rarely do for myself at all now, and I miss it even though the thing I miss is not actually shopping, but shopping with Mom, when I was young, before anything happened. Normal adult shopping is something I will never actually do, because it's no more possible for me to go shopping like normal adults do than it is for a man with no legs to wake up one day and walk. I can't miss shopping like you'd miss things you once had. I miss it in a different way. I miss it like you would miss a train.

I give a list to Vicky once a week; that's how I get what I need. Stores where I live are as big as college campuses. But sometimes I'll get stir-crazy, and I'll start to resent that I can't put my life through the same paces everybody else takes for granted. So I'll go out in the morning, out the door by nine o'clock at the latest, and I'll substitute the liquor store for the supermarket, since early-riser liquor store shoppers are people who wouldn't raise their eyes to you if you had a gun pointed at them. Besides which, I have a special place in my heart for the Pomona liquor stores that face the empty boulevards. I grew up in them, kind of: they used to have comic racks.

I needed to stock up on candy. I don't like asking Vicky to buy as much candy as I actually want to eat; I am ashamed about my candy habit. I will eat it until I feel sick. Once I get to the candy rack I can't control myself; I buy chewy Swee-Tarts and Red Hot Dollars, and I buy Magic Colors bubble gum cigarettes, which I like even though they don't have any actual taste at all. I go home and I eat them all straight from the bag while watching *The People's Court* or something, and I make noises like an octopus feeding underwater.

I pulled into the liquor store parking lot in the warm early-summer air and I took one of those big yoga breaths the rehab techs encourage you to take when they think your spirits are sinking. I went in, and I brought a good haul of candy up to the counter, about twenty dollars' worth. When I paid for it the clerk didn't even look up. I had a memory as I passed the dirty magazines by the front door, but I tamped it down. I looked away toward the sun still coming up over the Carl's Jr. across the street.

Coming back around the side of the store to the parking lot, I saw some teenagers hanging out in the bed of a white Toyota pickup. They must have pulled up while I was inside. They were smoking cigarettes in the deliberate self-conscious way of smoking teenagers: two of them, long-hairs. They were also openly watching me as I carried my bag toward the car. People like me prefer teenagers to other people. They are not afraid to stare.

The taller of the two, sandy blond hair and a wispy mustache on his upper lip, popped himself out and over the side of the truck like an athlete landing a long jump, and stopped himself when I'd thought he was going to come directly at me. "Dude!" he said, lifting his head. It was early. I felt good. Usually I ignore the few people who call out to me when I'm in public, but I looked over toward him and lifted my head right back.

"Yeah," I said.

"Dude, your *face*," he said.

I read a book called *Stardance* when I was thirteen years old. It left a big impression on me, though it's hard to say exactly how, since I don't remember much about the plot. It had something to do with zero gravity and people dancing in space, maybe in order to communicate something to an alien race. It is probable that when I remember *Stardance*, I am inventing several details as I go along.

Still, it was *Stardance*, or my memories of it, the ones I can either access or manufacture, that exploded momentarily in my mind just then as my eyes looked out from under the bulging reconstructed folds of skin that seem to hold them in place. I thought of dancers up in space, trying to stop aliens from enslaving or destroying the earth. I was turning the key in the lock on the car door but it felt like a kind of dancing to me.

"Dude, come here," said the sandy blond with the mustache. "Not trying to be a dick, just . . . can I see?" He blew a little smoke and turned his head off to the side as he did it; I saw this as a gesture of deference, of trying to make me see that he wasn't blowing smoke in my direction. It may have been, though I wonder, that he thought smoke might hurt my skin, which has a fresh-scraped look to it at all times.

Nobody ever asks me if they can look at my face. Except doctors and nurses, I mean. People do look at it, quite often, but usually only if they can convince themselves that I won't notice they're looking. They try not to let their eyes stop wandering when they look over in my direction; they pose as if they were surveying some broader scene. I understand, a little, the social dictate to not stare at misshapen people: you want to spare their feelings. You don't want them to feel ugly. At the same time, though, even before I became what I am, I used to wonder: Isn't it OK to stare if something seems to stand out? Why *not* stare? My own perspective is probably tainted by having spent long hours before mirrors after the accident. It would be pretty hard to make me feel "ugly." Words like *pretty* and *ugly* exist in a different vocabulary from the one you might invent to describe a face that had to be put back together by a team of surgeons. My face is strange and terrible. It merits a little staring.

If I were to scream right now, these two would jump straight out of their skins. Just open up my mouth as wide as it will go and start shrieking. Watch them run or freeze in place or just start screaming right back. These urges are still present sometimes. They rise and pop like bubbles on the surface of a bog, and then they're gone. They don't trouble me. They are voices from a distant past. "Sure," I said. I set my bag of candy in the car and I walked across the parking lot toward their truck.

We talked for a long time. The guy who'd called me over was named Kevin and his friend was named Steve, and Kevin said the Koreans at the liquor store were known to not card anybody who had a mustache. He slapped a brown bag in his flatbed as he said this and the full cans of beer gave off a muted *thunk*. I told him that when I was a little younger than he was now, we didn't even bother to try buying, because the owners knew our parents: we would chug beers off in a corner of the store behind the dusty greeting cards. Steve laughed and said they still had that greeting card rack in there and I told him I knew, that the cards in it were the exact same ones from when I was his age. Kevin offered me a beer. I told him I couldn't without a straw, and the quiet that fell onto the conversation for the next few seconds was like a great canyon in a desert landscape. Steve reached inside the window of the truck and flipped on the stereo, and the radio came on. It was KLOS. They were playing "Renegade" by Styx.

Kevin crushed his cigarette underneath his shoe and came

close enough to me to really get a good look, and he asked me if I was sure this was OK. It would be hard for me to describe how badly I wanted to smile. I could imagine myself in his position, out there on the other side of me, confronted with the scars and the shapes, all the lines that look like they were left on the canvas by a careless or distracted hand. What are we frightened of? Things that can't hurt us at all. I told him it was fine, it was kind of cool, that most people don't even ask when you can tell they want to. He looked up from the stretch of former cheekbone he'd been scrutinizing to make eye contact and he smiled, I think because he understood that I was telling him I thought he was brave. Steve stepped up behind him but kept a little distance. Two might have been too many.

But Kevin waved him over and Steve leaned in, and Kevin drew his index finger toward the recessed pit that lies due right of where my old nose was, and he held the tip of his finger near enough to the surface for me to feel his warmth, and said, "Bullet wound?" in a rhythm so casual that I felt like we were old friends, or coworkers, and I corrected him, saying: "Exit wound." They both gave half-nods and kept craning their eyes around the broad surface before them: down the side, cresting the ear, banking back over above and across the chin, their slowly moving heads like lunar landers.

I got a good look at them while they were circling me as respectfully and surgically as they could: they were a living tableau of denim with some stray silver accents here and there—rings, necklaces. They gave off a vague throb of energy, like thermal images of people on a screen. I recognized that throb. Once I'd held it inside myself, just barely. I felt comfortable with them. So I asked them whether my face freaked them out; I put it exactly like that, because I felt as if I was among members of my tribe. "Does it freak you out, my fucked-up face?" I said.

I don't really talk like that anymore. Those words, their sound, that summery lilt: all these came from somewhere in the past, or a buried part of the present. Whatever it was—past or present, or unknown future—it seemed to rise from the asphalt like a little invisible cyclone, swirling up around me in my mind. I felt like a panel in a comic book. In a different world, I might have looked like Kevin and Steve instead of like myself. I might have been buying beer and not candy, and smoking Marlboro reds, loitering in the parking lot and waiting for something to happen. The one constant in both possibilities was the liquor store, the parking lot. All roads leading to this quiet, empty place.

Steve answered first. "Well, dude," he said, and something in his tone made me want to cry for joy, "it is for sure fucked up, your face. But actually it's freakier before you see it up close. Up close, it's like . . ." He wasn't sure how to finish the thought.

"It's like tire tread," I offered.

Among the three of us I thought I felt a kinship. Sometimes I think I feel a bond when it's only my imagination. I'm used to that. But they laughed about the tire tread comparison, and they lit new cigarettes and offered one to me, which I accepted, and it gave me a head rush so strong that my vision washed out and I saw nothing but pulsing yellow for half a minute, and the song on the radio switched over from "Renegade" to "Even the Losers" as they asked me what was the worst part about having taken a bullet to the face and I said it was actually the way it messes up your hearing, which is true. We had a long discussion then: If you could have your face back or your hearing, you'd take your hearing? Yeah, I'm pretty sure I would. But you can still hear stuff, right? Yeah, but it comes in over a constant throbbing hum that keeps me awake at night sometimes. But seriously? You wouldn't rather look more normal?

This was Steve's exact phrase: *more normal*. It registered with me so suddenly, so immediately. I felt a kind of bliss. I wanted to hold Steve like a child. It's freakier before you see it up close. It's like tire tread. It's like a shag rug. It's like rope burn scars; it's like a badly paved road; it's like bent wheel spokes pressed into taffy. I told him the truth: that I didn't know; that I didn't know anymore if I wanted to be more normal or not. I had stopped being normal so early that it was hard to imagine being any other way than the way I was. This *was* normal for me. As far as I could tell, except on days when something went wrong with the routine, I lived a normal life.

Steve looked at Kevin and Kevin looked at Steve and they both said, "Normal life!" while touching their beer cans together like wineglasses, only at waist level, so that no car going past the tucked-away-between-buildings little liquor store parking lot would be able to see them. You know: in case a cop went past. I understood this right away, at some basic level, without having to ask. And this was the source of my bliss, my total quiet contentment: that we were three people who, if it came down to it, could communicate with one another using only gestures.

In the natural course of the conversation I ended up telling them about Carrie and Lance and they asked me if I was going to go to jail. I told them jail wasn't really on the table, but there was a good chance I'd end up going broke. Kevin told me he sort of knew how I felt, because his mom had kicked him out of the house a while back, and he'd had to sleep in the car until he got up the courage to call his dad. It had taken him a week to do it. He asked his dad if he could stay over at his house until he could save up enough money for first and last and security deposit. He had known that was the most he could ask. His dad didn't really have any money.

The sun was bright by now. Sometimes you feel like such an old man. For example, when you ask young men what they figure they'll do with their lives. And you see the look on their faces that says *What the fuck are you even talking about*, but they're not saying it to you, they're bouncing it off each other using a complicated system of facial tics and gestures, which they know they can do because you probably don't get it. Which is what makes me different: I *do* get it. I see the gestural sema-phore and can read it without having to think twice about it. It is an excruciatingly painful thing to see and feel, so I try to avoid it, but I sensed some connection with Steve and Kevin, so I asked them what they figured they were going to do, you know, after summer, maybe.

Steve said, "Fuck if I know," and Kevin said, "I'm going to stay as high as I can," and they bumped fists and then at the exact same moment raised their free hands flat into the air, their palms toward me. They were asking me to give them the high five. I gave them the high five. I felt like the sun had just risen inside me.

"What about you, though, dude?" said Steve. "What the fuck are you going to do?"

I knew what I was going to say; I paused for effect. "I'm going to go home and eat candy and stay high as long as I can," I said.

Kevin and Steve said staggered *No doubt*s, automatically, reflexively, but then Kevin said: "That whole court thing, though, dude. What are you going to do?" He pulled at his beer.

"Fuck 'em," I said. When I pronounce the letter *f*, I spit. Neither of them flinched. I thought a little about Carrie's parents, to whom I usually bore no particular ill will, because I always try to put myself in the other guy's shoes. If I had a kid who killed herself because she'd gotten confused about some game she was playing with some stranger far away, I'd hate that stranger, too. That is usually how I think. But I said it again, and I meant it. "Fuck 'em."

Again Steve and Kevin thunked their beer cans together. "Fuck 'em!" they said, in near unison. I smiled my horrible smile.

8 I felt so terrible when Carrie died. Trying to explain the feeling I had is like trying to describe what you see when your eyes are bandaged: it's not impossible, but it's different from describing something you can actually look at, something you might see in the course of a normal day. It is trying to describe something at which you are unable to look directly.

She never wrote to me as often as Lance did; it was usually him writing the letters and signing on behalf of them both. They played as a team: L+C, two capital initials with a plus sign in between. In the margins of their letters, sometimes, or after the sign-off, she would also write something. Or if somehow Lance had been sidelined. One July, when his family took him down to Branson on vacation, for example: that was the week when Carrie sent in a turn so there'd be news for Lance when he came home. *L is on vacation so I thought if I make a move & it's good he will be excited when he comes home so here it is I know all turns are final but please don't let me do something stupid we have so much fun together*, she wrote. She had decided to have the two of them hide behind a dumpster until the sun went down, because it was hot in the town through which they were passing, and the mutants who had overrun the town were carnivorous and could smell less keenly once the air got cool.

I'd sent her a little note in reply. It was both sweet and painful to me to think of how much L+C meant to each other, how their lives seemed almost made for each other. When I was in high school, I'd only ever had two girlfriends: one for almost no time at all—two weeks early in freshman year, at the way station between junior high and the new social order being established at high school—and Kimmy for even less time than that, really just an unsure day or two right before the accident. Technically, I guess, she had still been my girl-friend when she visited me in my bandages at the hospital, but those visits were of a different order. I understood a little about how good it must feel to have someone who loves you out there in the wilds of high school; for a few days I'd known what that was like, too. But what Kimmy meant to me in the aftermath was something different and higher, a singular thing in the world with no readily available points of comparison. She was just sixteen, but she had the stomach to stand near a smoking wreck.

On the Xeroxed move I took from the file cabinet, I wrote: *Good work to both of you Carrie. It's safe behind the dumpster. Tell Lance when he gets home that you kept him from harm.* I remember feeling a little guilty, because while it's possible to make a move that kills off your character within the game, it's almost never possible to walk straight into a fatal trap; telling somebody their game is over is a bad business move, and I'd known that before I ever took out the first ad. So staying put until dark was a good move, one that would advance the player painlessly toward the short-term objective of reaching the city limit unharmed; there was no real danger. But the wrong move could have delayed the team until winter, scaling hospital exteriors to get at the one uncontaminated bottle of disinfectant or a snakebite kit. There was a colony of snakes in the ditch just a few hundred yards away: she might have chosen HEAD FOR THE DITCH instead of REST BY THE DUMPSTER. So I hadn't lied. I had just played up the bright side.

When Lance got home and sent in his moves, he was excited. I remember his excitement, how I could see it in the way the pencil dug into the page. I was piecing together what I knew about him while picking out clothes for the hearing. Vicky had come in to help me dress. I didn't need her help—I can dress myself—but I was grateful. Sometimes I wondered what Vicky made of my work, since she never asked me about it and I didn't usually volunteer much; our conversations stuck mainly to simple things like food or the weather or how we were feeling. She told me about her family sometimes. If she found me at my work she mostly left me at it.

It was difficult, that day, to remain in the moment. I wanted her to know how I felt, thinking of Lance where he was now: in a place called Casa Central, some physical rehabilitation center for adolescents. Most of his fellow patients had survived more sudden traumas than his: car accidents, house fires. His problems had a better shot at total resolution, but in the immediate present they were as bad as anybody's. He'd spent days down in a shallow pit without food, with only forming ice to suck for water. Now he lay on a burn recovery bed all day hoping that feeling would return to his legs from the knees down, his face salved and wrapped, everybody praying that enough attention would encourage some of the skin to grow back.

As best as I can put it together, this is what I can tell you about Lance Patterson: he was born to a couple in their mid-twenties who had been married for several years. His father worked the evening shift at some Winter Park assembly line that made parts for machines; his mother was a substitute in the grade schools. His family was a good family; they weren't rich, but they all lived together and stayed in one place. Of course I only knew him through the mail, but I imagined him as an awkward boy with too much energy. His teachers liked him, and they told him so; I know this because he mentioned it once when he said that the other kids his age didn't like him but his teachers were nice. He spent his afternoons after school hanging around the house, watching television and keeping himself entertained. He had a few friends, all casual, but was personally somewhat guarded; when Carrie came into his life, a corner of the world he'd only ever dreamed about was opened for him. I learned about this corner of his world when he brought her into the game, which he'd only been playing for a few months. *Is it OK if I have a partner playing with me who can just start where I'm at?* he wrote. *Can we just say I found her hiding somewhere?* I didn't see why not; I couldn't write a special turn for it, but I wrote at the top of his next turn: *You have been joined by a young technician who can help you tap the aquifer.*

He was not unusual in sending me bits and pieces of his life; that, in part, was what contributed to my horror at the whole situation. There might have been others like him about whom I'd never heard, people whose play had taken them into lightless hallways: What of them? They found their way out and disappeared. Or they never said anything and kept on playing. What did I know about these people, about anybody anywhere whom disaster hadn't struck? There was Chris, he was all right. But generally the only way we ever know anything about anything is if something goes wrong. Knowing this is hard for me.

"This is a picture of a boy named Lance," I said to Vicky, out of nowhere, while she was straightening things up. "He plays that game you always see me working on." I felt like a man leaving a spaceship for the surface of a new planet; it is pretty rare for me to feel that sort of need so many seem to have, that irresistible desire to tell somebody else what they're thinking. I hadn't talked to Vicky about the lawsuit; for several reasons I tend to keep my conversations with people limited to basic, pleasant things like the weather or which kind of macaroni and cheese tastes the best.

"Oh?" said Vicky. Back in my own trauma ward days I knew several social workers who could have learned a thing or two about reflective listening from Vicky.

"Yeah," I said. She was making my bed for me hospital style, tight corners and accordion folds. "He's in the hospital now but he's been playing Trace Italian for almost three years. Him and his girlfriend. She died."

"I'm real sorry," she said, "to hear it." I could see her taking the measure of me, noticing how talkative I was today. "How is he getting by, now?"

"He's—" I looked for the word, and for a few seconds while I looked, I considered her question, the depths of understanding that seemed to have formed its words: How many people had she taken care of whose problems involved getting by or not getting by in so many hundreds of different degrees? "He's managing," is what I came up with. She came over and sat down beside me, getting her dressing-changing things together on a tray, and she waited for me to continue.

"He went a long time without food or enough clothes to keep him warm," I said. "He was in a place a long way from his home and he didn't know how cold it got there, and by the time he figured it out, it was too late. He tried to save his girl-friend, they say, but she was trying to save him, too, and she didn't make it. They liked to read the same books together, and see the same movies and talk about them; he used to write to tell me about the things they liked to think about. I don't think he really knows how to think a few steps ahead, you know."

"Young people can't think ahead," she said. She was open-ing up some Betadine swabs.

I laughed my little wet throat-laugh. "I know," I said; "you know I know. I keep hoping he won't blame himself too much for being stupid. I mean, he is a little stupid, I think, but to me that's not a bad thing to say about a person. I'm a little stupid but I'm all right. Lance is young and stupid though, I guess. That's two strikes."

"Now, now," said Vicky.

"He likes to play video games but he hasn't got any sensation in the pads of his fingers anymore so he can't feel them pressing on the buttons, and he says it feels weird, so the games aren't as fun. The first thing he thought of when his girlfriend died was what she'd want him to do, how to keep the memory of her happy in his imagination. What a sweet kid," I said. My face stung. "They met in junior high school band; she played the flute, I guess, and he was in the drum section, and they went to the movies together a lot." I wanted to give Lance a better biography, but all l really had at the ready were some bare bits and details: the parts he hadn't been able to stop himself from mentioning, the pieces of himself that flew from him naturally like sparks from a torch.

"Well, he sounds like a nice boy," said Vicky, straightening my collar for me. The sun was cresting the cypresses that line the walkway, and a clean warm light had filled the room. It's hard not to feel good in that kind of light. I nodded, and I looked at her and felt such gratitude to have her around. I was happy to know her in my small, formal, dependent way. And I felt a ravenous grief for nice boys who are too stupid to take care of themselves, and too dumb to remember to check the surrounding brush for snakes before settling down to sleep for the night.

9 They freeze up when I open the door. You can see it happen. They're in a sort of imagined forward motion, ready to launch into whatever pitch they've come to give, and then the sight of me arrests them mid-swing. Wielding this kind of power feels different from what I imagine people who crave power think they'll get if they ever get their wish. Because this . . . this can't be what people want. Or maybe it is, and I just don't really understand how power works, I think sometimes. But then I think about it some more, and I think: Yes, I do know something about what power is, how it works. What it's like. I do know.

"Sean Phillips?" is what the process server said, already holding up the summons in front of his face like a shield. He was in his early twenties. I don't think anyone had warned him about adjusting his expectations. Probably he was working through a whole sheaf of cases, nameless after a few hours on the clock, one indistinguishable from the next. I assume that you end up seeing all sorts of people in the course of your workday in a job like this; in any job, really. But "all sorts of people," in most lives, is a spectrum with fairly narrow extremes. If your job involves knocking on doors, your parameters might begin on the far end with a man who answers his motel room door naked and dripping wet, and on the other side you might find some guy who tries to tip you when you leave. If you go out on religious work, I imagine you learn early that some people are glad to see you and other people are mad. I am different; I'm outside all that. People don't expect to meet me. They don't know they have expectations, but I show them by counterexample what their expectations were. I had old music from my teenage years playing loud on the stereo when the process server found himself having to decide whether to look at me or not.

I always wonder if people are afraid of me because they think I'll do something: press my face up against them, or start making funny noises. I am always a little tempted to satisfy their fears. But I never do it; it would feel wrong; it would be wrong. I don't need to make myself feel better by frightening people or making them squirm. When I was a child, I dreamed of powers like these, but I no longer have those dreams. I am free.

I said, "Sean Phillips last time I checked," as clearly and lightly as I could, and I grabbed the pen from his outstretched hand. I heard him say "If you could just sign here," but I was already ahead of him. I pictured the scene between us, how it couldn't have been an easy combination: the door opening, me there, the loud, unpleasant music blaring away and forcing him to raise his voice for his one big line. So I signed quickly, and when he'd left, I read the summons. And then I read it again. That's what you do when something like this starts to happen in your life: you check and recheck to see if it's real.

And you start talking out loud to yourself, trying to explain it, seeing if you really understand. You then get angry. I did, anyway; I wanted to knock something over. Old feelings, long pressed down to where they couldn't do any more harm, shed weight and rose inside me like vapor. They felt, to me, the way ghosts are supposed to look. They came up through the center of my body until I felt them at the back of my throat, tendriling out onto my tongue from way down in there. But they did not escape. I pressed the nail of my right index finger into the pad of my thumb rhythmically and focused on the dull sharpness bearing down while waiting for the feeling to ease.

Dear Freak,

With the internet now we can find out all about you so we don't have to write to your PO box. We know where you live. So don't think you are safe because you aren't safe from the people who loved Lance and Carrie and took their lifes SERIOUSLY and you will never be safe. Die in a hole, X.

There'd been bad news in the mail all week, but mixed in with it there'd been regular mail, plain mail: Stray moves from early Trace denizens, subscription renewals. Insurance statements I didn't usually read because they always said the same thing: Your coverage continues at the level of care from the preceding period; please advise us immediately of any change in status, etcetera. Month after month. A few bills. And junk mail. Vitamin catalogs. Supplements. None of it could numb the live wires I kept grabbing every other time I split an envelope open: Carrie dead. Lance sure to lose a foot, maybe both, maybe a hand, maybe both of those, too. Large sections of his face blackened by frostbite. His fever rendering him delirious. Fund-raisers at their parents' churches, flyers for bake sales, clippings from Florida papers with names circled or underlined twice. And Lance and Carrie's friends, writing to tell me either that they blamed me for what had happened, or else that they didn't and wouldn't no matter what anyone said; or just to tell me about what their friends were like, how they'd been in real life, how painful it was to know that all that was changed. And now this: a single page, a form, advising me in dry language that a hearing was to be held to determine where fault, if any, rested in the matter of, etcetera, wherefore my presence was required, and could be compelled if not given voluntarily, etcetera, wherefore the recipient should contact, at the following number without delay, etcetera.

My parents arranged all kinds of meetings with people back when they were running around looking for answers. I don't remember them much, aside from a stray scene or two that stick with me like memorable sequences from otherwise forgotten films. These few short clips are interesting to me, and I can stand them now, but there was a time when I blocked them out. People trying to help you when you're past help are raw and helpless. Nobody wins: you get nothing; they feel worse. I mainly remember the feeling among us when the hearings and meetings were finally all over: Dad growing distant, detached. Mom finding the quiet mask from which her face would never fully emerge again.

They held on to their anger until after they'd exhausted their leads; then it was gone. I don't know what they replaced it with. Something, I figure. I feel guilt, and sympathy, and shame, and I share it with them in letters I don't mail, because the people who need to read those letters are also gone. They vanished into a meeting room one day and were never seen again.

I stood in the kitchen by the window reading the summons; it was so boring. The facts that had brought it into being were the stuff of nightmares, vivid and awful and real, but the thing that came to speak of them was a lifeless sequence of instructions written in a language no one alive even spoke. Nobody talks like that. People only talk like that when they can't stand to tell you what they mean. I lead a sane and quiet life: the sun shone on the grape-candy purple jacaranda in the breezeway outside, and the oleander and the bottlebrush were in bloom down the walkway, and I felt like I had been suddenly shot out into space, the world I'd left behind terrible and frightening, only now I couldn't breathe at all. I felt my blood quickly becoming starved of oxygen and my cells beginning to swell, and the stars around me grew brighter and then faded, and then nothing happened at all, and I stood by the window a while longer with the summons in my hand, wanting to run back to the front door to watch the process server get back into his car but knowing I'd missed him already, feeling the instinct to run to the door emerge anyway as a genuine urgency in my thin, underdeveloped legs.

The noise can't really be blocked, just bested. Music therapists play you droning synthesizer music or classical when you're in physical rehab; music therapists are the sweetest people; of all the people who try to help you in the hospital, they're the ones whose faith in their power to heal seems strongest. But it takes high-pitched sounds with a thick texture and a persistent rhythm to really make the *whoosh* go away. Bamboo flutes can't touch it. Neither did the stuff my friends and I had all been listening to together ever since we'd started hanging out, the blues-rock stadium stuff. And that was how I got into blindly ordering strange music through the mail: *Spirit of Cimmeria* always had one or two ads for music "inspired by the genius of Robert E. Howard," for example—stuff made by guys living in distant backwaters with no hope of ever making their voices heard anywhere, writing songs about the books they spent all their free time reading just trying to escape, playacting in a vacuum. There were similar ads in comic books, in *Omni.* They were everywhere if you knew how to look, so I spent my allowance on this kind of thing. Mom still gave me an allowance, even after what I'd done.

The first tape I got was folk music from someplace in Massachusetts, and I hated it. The second, which I'd ordered on the same day as the first one but which took a week longer to arrive, was by a band called Sunlight, and it came from Texas. I remember being excited about that, because Robert E. Howard was from Texas: he blew his brains out in the driveway of his house in Cross Plains. He was thirty years old and his mother was in a coma. I memorized all these details when I was fourteen, running around everywhere devouring every piece of information about Conan I could find; it had a religious appeal for me.

Sunlight's tape was called *In Hyborian Sleep* and by normal standards it sounded terrible: there were no bass frequencies, the singer just screamed, the drums were a constant artillery barrage the whole time. But it transported me. It freed me from the ringing in my ears and from the decision that sound was always pointing toward, from what the sound meant. From the second its staticky blasts started scratching through the speakers of my cheap Montgomery Ward stereo, I loved it, and I turned it up as loud as I could get it to go without distorting. I held my big head in the sweet spot between the speakers and closed my eyes to dream of barbarian conquest, and that's how Mom found me when she came in.

I think I was half-conscious of her for a minute: something from outside the squall trying to draw me out. "Sean, please!" was the first thing I heard.

I turned the music down but not off. "Please what?" I said.

"Please tell me what it means that you're listening to such . . ." I could see the tension in her neck, in her eyebrows. "Such racket."

"What it means?" I said. It was still early in the whole process; I always felt humiliated if a situation called for an answer of more than a few words, and I could feel my anger building.

"Sean," she said, "we . . ." and then she stopped herself again. Over the years I have tried to figure out what thoughts, what actual words, lay in the gaps between the things my mother starts to say and the things she ends up saying. "Whatever this is, it's too much. You're alone in your room all the time, and the music's always on, and you're still doing that Conan thing you did when you were just a—"

I saw my mother's eyes fill halfway with tears. She held out her hand in an almost stage-like gesture, and swept it from left to right in an arc that drew in the stereo, the fanzines, the books and cassettes piled on top of the turntable's dust cover, and the Michael Whelan posters on the walls that my dad had taken down while I'd been away, which I'd dug right back out and hung again as soon as I got home. And the sketches I'd made of the Plague Blaster gun: those were up now, too, taped to the walls in places of prominence. These were big improvements over the nylon lariats the Retrievers had used in earlier drafts of the Trace outline. They fit right in your hand. They were thumbtacked in clusters on the wall next to the bed, one on top of another: the guns, and the Retrievers, and the mutated horses they rode through Kansas on. The sketches and maps clustered out and overlapped with one another like flyers on telephone poles. Mom let her hand drop back to her side, and she said, "It's just too much, honey," and I couldn't look her in the eye.

I wish now that I could have explained to her about the noise in my head and the music fixing it, but I couldn't, because it all happened too quickly and my temper flared before I had a chance to think. I punched the POWER button on the stereo to shut the whole thing off at once and all the life went out of it, and the noise roared in my ears again, worse than ever. I sat on my bed and looked down at the floor, and my mother came and sat next to me and put her arm over my shoulder, buddy-style. I leaned into her, against her, feeling sorry now, regret rushing in to fill the spaces where the anger drained. "It's OK, I'm sorry," she said. In the corner of my eye I caught the Plague Blaster, its contours clean, its heft exactly right.

I stopped listening to tapes at some point: it was a phase. You either get used to noises in your head, or you learn to focus instead on whatever other noises happen to be present in the room, like the air conditioner. Still, I kept them, and they're arranged neatly on top of the dresser in my bedroom, which means Vicky dusts them once a week. They look like museum pieces now. *Chaos Blood, Black Lake, Rexecutioner's Dream.* Sean at sixteen thought *Rexecutioner's Dream* was the greatest thing he'd ever heard, something so strange and different it seemed like a message from another realm. It had cover art, but the art was glued onto the inner sleeve of a standard-issue blank cassette; the spine was hand lettered. It was the product of someone's hard work, a vision brought into the world of real things. A dream disguised in a crude, plain package.

When the hate mail started up I had an impulse of the sort I rarely get anymore, the kind the antidepressants I'm supposed to be taking would probably keep completely and indefinitely in check. I was sitting up in bed reading the postcard that began *You aren't going to hear us when we come in you ugly reject,* trying to see if reading it several times over would quiet the real fear that it gave me—*You're just going to feel the pain*—and the light through the window caught the edge of something hard and shiny across the room, and I thought, if any of these have a return address in them, I'm going to send that person a tape. Something random from on top of the dresser. *Fire Caverns.* Just put it into a Jiffy bag and mail it.

I got as far as sliding one of the tapes out from the row and setting it down on my desk next to the letters, like an arrow in the quiver. But of course nobody threatening to kill me was about to send a return address. *I hope they give you the chair.*

And then I pictured myself sending some incomprehensible tape to a stranger whose hatred for me was a pure flame, bright and clear: someone who'd hear a package drop in through his mail slot one day and find, when he opened it, this unexpected, undecodable *thing*. And he'd turn it over in his hands, trying to make sense of it, and he'd feel all shaken up. Or confused. Or a little scared. And I said out loud: "No," and did the deep breathing exercises I learned in relaxation class when I was seventeen. I made ready to tear the threats all into neat squares, but instead I put them in a manila envelope and tucked it into the bottom drawer in the filing cabinet, down among the scenes and byroads almost no one's ever seen.

More mail came in the following weeks; I wondered if swells in volume meant there'd been some editorial in a local paper somewhere about a gunshot survivor who'd lured a couple of teenagers to a frozen grave. Maybe even a human-interest story on the evening news. Because it did seem to come in waves. There were appeals to my conscience to "turn myself in," and prayer groups letting me know they were interceding with God on my behalf. I stopped reading this stuff fairly quickly; I either filed them or, if an envelope looked a little fat and came from an unknown source, I'd hand it over unopened to my lawyer, who I assume put them all into a filing cabinet of her own. But *Dear Freak* was the first one, out ahead of the actual news, a confusing and frightening intrusion into the dull quiet of my life, the first I had heard about any of this. The crazy road trip letters from Lance and Carrie had stopped suddenly, and I'd thought maybe their parents had made them come home; then there'd been radio silence for a week—two weeks— and then, *Dear Freak, With the internet now*, one of about

seven letters from strangers that came that day, some support-
ive and some caustic, a stack around which the postman or
somebody at the post office had put a rubber band. I remember the rubber band because I reflexively threaded it from my
pinkie around my thumb to my index finger pistol-style and
shot it across the room.

10

I was cleaning out the bathroom cabinets when I ran across the expired medications . . . they were tucked back in a corner. They formed a little squadron of yellow-brown bottles, hidden away from view. When I uncovered them their serial numbers and expiration dates met the incoming light like bits of unearthed code on ancient tablets. I had no conscious memory of hiding the bottles back there, away from sight; maybe they'd been getting pushed back gradually over the years, until at some point they reached a place where they were safe from scrutiny. But they were all upright, like orderly sentries, which worked somewhat against that theory.

There was a small, strange moment during which I had this feeling that someone was filming me, which was ridiculous, but it was that specific—"there's a camera on me"—and then some hard ancient pushed-down thing, a thing I'd felt or thought or feared a long time ago, something I'd since managed to sheathe in an imaginary scabbard inside myself, erupted through its casing like a bursting cyst. I had to really struggle to recover. Something was dislodging itself, as from a cavern inside my body or brain, and this situation seemed so divorced from waking reality that my own dimensions lost their power to persuade. I craned my great head and saw all that yellow-brown plastic catch the light, little pills glinting like ammunition, and then my brain went to work, juggling and generating several internal voices at once: someone's filming this; this isn't real; whoever Sean is, it's not who I think he is; all the details I think I know about things are lies; somebody is trying to see what I'll do when I run across these bottles; this is a test but there won't be any grade later; the tape is rolling but I'm never going to see the tape. It is a terrible thing to feel trapped within a movie whose plot twists are senseless. This is why people cry at the movies: because everybody's doomed. No one in a movie can help themselves in any way. Their fate has already staked its claim on them from the moment they appear onscreen.

I looked away; I looked away. Held myself steady for a second and then got back to the work of the cleaning, shaking free of the crazy feelings, and I felt the corners of my mouth, half smiling. Most people can clean their bathroom cabinets without waking up any traumatic memories. Not me, not yet, I guess. But as Dave the art therapist told me once when he found me sulking: it's not so bad to be special. My journey, he said, was longer and slower. He looked me in the eyes, which impressed me, and told me that my good fortune was to learn what special really meant.

I raised my spray bottle, filled with plain white vinegar solution, and I blasted the mirror cheerfully, wiping the glass with a wadded newspaper until the vinegar dried. Then I sank an easy two into the wastebasket on the other side of the toilet, and I reached back into the cabinet without thinking too hard. I set the old medication bottles down on the counter one at a time, and after I'd finished clearing out the rest of the cabinet, I took a closer look at them.

I was eleven, maybe twelve, I'm not completely sure, when I was given a small black-and-white television and told I could keep it in my room. My grandmother had just died; she was my mother's mother, and she'd lived most of her life in one house, just a mile or so away from where we settled when we finally circled back to Montclair. When she died, she left behind a room all full of grandma things, things too familiar to be given to Goodwill but too yellowed to be kept out in plain view. In the wake of her death a small windfall came my way. Besides the television, I got two transistor radios; a blanket that smelled, as I would later learn, like a hospital smells; and a hollow stone statue of an owl, which had been sitting atop the wall-mounted heater in my grandmother's room for as long as I could remember.

Both the owl and the television became immediate touchstones. I talked to the owl sometimes, and I'm not sure why; I don't remember what I told it or when I stopped doing it. I just remember that it was a thing I did for a while. The TV I used like a night-light. I plugged it in and left it on.

This was back in the age of networks and UHF. Most stations signed off sometime toward two in the morning. But on summer nights I'd stay awake until three, and sometimes later, because a pulsing feeling in my stomach made it hard for me to want to sleep. In my room down the hall with my face close to the bright screen, cross-legged. Close enough to the screen to describe variations in the grain of the dust that would form on the glass. Once in a while I'd wipe it clean with the palm of my hot, oily hand. I would watch anything; I believed everything. I could convince myself that I was the last person in the world, watching the screen after the station had signed off, sinking into the blur. Sometimes I'd fall asleep on the floor, my face in the carpet, and I'd wake up with the TV still on, my head near the speaker, local news droning. My mom would come in later, in the morning, and say it wasn't good for me, but how could I explain?

What I had on those nights were as near as I had come since childhood to religious experiences. Lots of people who survive personal traumas get close to God. My accident didn't do that for me. It was like a cleansing wind: mystic thoughts would always be hard to come by for me afterward. Those times of snowy vision I'd had in the summers after my grandmother died subsequently became the stuff of personal myth for me. My parents had their own version of it, which was linear; it told a story about me staying up late and reading things and watching things that told me to do something awful, of staring too long at a static screen. It's because they thought this, and because they maybe still do, that I can't communicate with them. I can't explain to them what those nights were like except to say that they gave me a sort of shelter. "Shelter from what?" they would say if I managed to put it to them that plainly. "Why did you need shelter?" Some things are hard to explain to your parents. Some things are hard to explain,

97

period, but your parents especially are never going to understand them.

All that was left of the Navane was a dark orange film, hard-
ened against the plastic walls of the dropper bottle, segmented
and flaking like dried earth. I remembered this stuff. It was
the worst of the worst. It came with all kinds of warnings
about going out into the sun and what to use on your skin to
protect yourself from the extra sensitivity, which seemed like
jokes to me, like they had to be meant as jokes. I think it was
years before I stood outside in the sun at all for longer than
the few minutes it took me to get from a transport van into
the cool shade of the indoors.

I sniffed at the bottle. There wasn't a whole lot of scent
left; just enough for me to grab hold of the memory of what it
had been like getting this stuff from the dropper to my tongue.
Like forcing a cadaver to drool something sweet into my mouth.
Whole sweeping narratives had formed inside me around this
medication, I remembered: stories I'd told myself to make taking it less numbing, to give not just meaning but intrigue to
my dull condition. Explorers on distant South American
mountainsides retrieving flowers from rock cliffs whose petals
alone could yield the essence that would make the nauseating
syrup in the tinted bottle: but you couldn't get the essence
directly from the petals; it was far too potent for human beings,
it'd kill you; first you had to feed it to sparrows, whose livers
filtered out the toxins, then cut out the livers and boil all the
remaining organs in water. Then you strained the resulting
decoction through cheesecloth and diluted it in a ten-to-one

solution, and capped the bottles you'd drained it into and kept them away from light, because what you were left with was thiothixene HCl, known commercially as Navane, which I took in oral suspension because the doctor thought without it I might see or hear bad things.

Every medication from the drawer had not just one story like this but several. Pale pink Tegretol hauled across the Caucasus by caravan under cover of night, the only man in the world capable of manufacturing it unaware that his creation was being packaged and sold to people in the hated nations of the West. Xanax, certifiably the medication that came from space, traded to the architects of our shadow government in exchange for a full map of human DNA, the eventual future costs of this trade arrangement unspoken but plain as day to everybody involved, a rash of suicides and disappearances cropping up when the uselessness of the medicine for anything beyond mild sedation was revealed. Ludiomil, the one the drug companies were lying to all the doctors about, telling them it did one thing when really it did another, all the while advising baffled treatment teams that one of Ludiomil's side effects was to make patients lie about how it made them feel; and so the doctors kept right on prescribing it to treat something it didn't really treat, blind actors in a study whose actual aim would never be known by anyone. I made up these stories when they brought me the medications with my breakfast, lunch, and dinner, and I refined them some after I'd been sent home. Everything became infused with purpose. It's hard to overstate how deep the need can get for things to make sense.

There was also Darvocet. Darvocet had some stories, too,

but unlike the others they were all true. I had learned them in real time: I'm burning from the neck up. Every repaired bone feels like it has been electrified. Every thought or emotion I have is focused on the pounding pain in my face, which feels as big as the side of a barn. I hurt so much that I would trade anything for relief, do anything, hurt anyone. I remember the day I tried to make a deal with the devil: how stupid I felt, how I cried to know there was no Satan to help me, how there was only the medication they'd give me when I couldn't pretend I didn't need it anymore. Which I tried to do all the time; I hated how much I needed all the help they gave me, hated needing to call the nurse, hated feeling like my greatest success would be in making childhood my permanent condition.

Somewhere in the middle of a long night, between one dosage of Darvocet and the next, I made a promise to myself. I remembered it now. I'd promised myself that all this was temporary, the medication and the bed in the room where the blinds were always down, and that I would get out of it somehow, get away somewhere, do something again with little reference to any of it. I didn't promise myself future success or total recovery. Just escape. I remember that it was dark in the room when I came up with the promise, and that I had a special way of wording it that I swore to myself I'd never forget, and I noticed, now, shaking the Darvocet bottle with a few tabs left in it, that of course I had forgotten whatever the special magic words of my promise had actually been. They had been scattered to the winds long since. I don't think I can explain why it made me happy to learn that I'd been unable to keep my promise to myself, but it did. I felt so content to have forgotten: like I'd been touched by a blessing so obscure that almost no one would ever share in it, or no one I'd ever know or hear about. Like I belonged to a tiny secret brotherhood of people who'd forgotten something hard.

I arranged the bottles into a loosely octagonal formation on the counter, and I pictured a very small person sitting at the center of the octagon, no bigger than the distal joint of my little finger, bored but safe, half-crazy from isolation but protected from the outside world. That person was me. My parents would have asked the younger me, what do you want to be safe from? After the accident nobody would ask. That was, to put it harshly, the best thing about the rifle blast that destroyed most of my face.

I saw a show about music one summer on that TV. I saw it twice.

They were showing it on TBN, the Trinity Broadcasting Network, "fifty thousand watts of power broadcasting from Costa Mesa, California"—I watched TBN a lot, because when all the other stations had powered down their transmitters for the night, TBN stayed on. After a while I started to notice patterns in the way they operated, and I came up with theories about how things worked at TBN. For example: sometimes you'd feel pretty certain you were seeing the same show twice, but I became convinced this was never actually true; maybe there'd be the same hosts and the same guests going over the same material, and it'd seem like you were watching the same thing you'd watched once already, but there were variations if you looked hard enough. I learned to look very hard.

Sometimes their voices would sound different, more strained or more awake, more tired or somewhat softer. Gradations in tone. And sometimes they'd just look less involved, a little more distracted, a little less believable. But everyone would still pretend the conversation hadn't already taken place, that all these questions hadn't already been answered to everybody's satisfaction.

And then sometimes, not often but for me always with a profound feeling of revelation, the conversation would go to a new place: not too far off the script, but somewhere just down a side path, for five minutes, maybe, or even less. Things would briefly open, and, in the opening, possibilities would emerge. Jan, with the high-piled hair, would remember something her mother used to say to her; or a guest would be reminded of a story he'd heard from somebody in his travels, and he'd lose the thread somewhere in the middle of the story but keep right on telling it. Or a musician from the in-studio band would say something like "That's the first time we've played that song in a while," but when you saw the same show again two nights later he'd say "We don't get to play that song as much as we used to" instead. Or a visiting preacher might swap out a story about his trip to Houston for another about his home parish in Phoenix. Or someone would carry out a Bible verse for an extra line or two, heading off into parts unknown before breaking abruptly off.

When I saw the music show the second time it seemed like there were more of these glitches than usual. The show was about Satanism in music: apparently bands had started encoding Satanic messages into their songs by recording the music backwards, and teenagers were being won over for Satan through this process. They had a couple of experts on the show as guests, and they said that rock music, which had become the most popular music in the world, was being used by the devil to get his message across. Does the devil actually have his own message? This seemed like a big question for me when I was thirteen and up late on summer nights.

They introduced one guest as a guy who'd been a rock musician for many years before he'd started living for the Lord. He was there to explain how the messages got put into rock music, whether it was something people did on purpose or some more subtle process from the spiritual world; his mission was to spell out what the messages meant in greater detail, because sometimes they were hard to understand, and it was important to know what was out there. "Some of the stuff that's out there," he said, "it's really amazing, what's right out there under your nose." He gave everybody a grave look, and they passed the same look around among themselves, and I felt, watching, like I was either missing out on something or being let in on a big secret: or someplace in the space between those two possibilities, drifting.

It was hard to follow, but as near as I could figure it, singers whose hearts were in the wrong place were vulnerable to demonic influence when they wrote. They wouldn't know when the process started, and it would take hold of them before they knew it: they became emissaries then, messengers carrying sealed envelopes. They sang songs they felt they'd written but actually hadn't, and if you played them backwards, they spread the message of Satan.

Nobody on the broadcast seemed particularly surprised by this claim. The world was a place full of ugly magic. As an example, the guest held up a record by a singer named Larry Norman, which he said was full of backwards messages: "packed" was the way he put it. Larry Norman made Christian music—"the so-called Christian rock," the guest practically spat—and he'd actually been a guest of Paul and Jan on the show at some point, which they mentioned with a look of concern. And then the guest told the producers to cue up a Larry Norman record, and they played it forward and then reversed it, and in reverse, it sounded like a hole opening up in the earth out in the dark, abandoned desert.

What you were supposed to hear when the record played backwards was the phrase *wolf in white van*. Nobody had a very firm idea of what that was supposed to mean, but they all agreed about what they were hearing: that it was a hellish picture to paint, and for young people to hear. Paul did ask what, exactly, it meant, and the guest talked about the symbol of the wolf in ancient cultures, but nothing got much clearer. It was a dark smudge of an idea shared among believers.

The second time I saw the show it looked like everybody'd kept right on worrying about the whole question between the first broadcast and its twin. They seemed tired, and a little frightened, and they were beginning to repeat themselves, working the meaningless backwards phrases out loud like riddles nobody could quite solve. It took them longer to get from one point to the next; the messages were sticking in their throats, looming before them like visions. That was when I got the idea, because the prayer line number was right there on the screen.

In the hallway there was a phone with a long cord. Mom and me were alone in the house all weekend; Dad was off hunting boar with his friends from work up in Solano County like he did every summer. The house felt so different with fewer people in it. It was the middle of the night; I crept out of my room quietly, and I snuck the phone down the short distance from its little hallway alcove to my room, and I threaded the cord through the gap between the door and the carpet so it wouldn't get pinched in the jamb. I eased the door shut, and I wondered why I was doing this, but at the same time I felt like it was too late to turn back.

"Praise the Lord, this is Carol," said the woman on the other end when the line picked up. I always remembered that afterward, the exact sound and rhythm: "Praise the Lord, this is Carol." Was I younger then than I now believe I was? I told her my name was Sean, and that I had a question for the guest.

Carol laughed. "This isn't our call-in show, honey," she said, gently. "That's that morning show, on the weekdays."

"I just had a question," I said. For a minute neither of us said anything and I could hear the other operators praying with callers in the background.

"I know, honey, but they can't really—" She stopped for a second. "What's your question, hon?" she said.

What I'd meant to ask her was why the devil would talk backwards: why he didn't just get his message out directly, by speaking clearly, straight into the brains of the people he knew he could win over. To me this was obviously the most important question about the whole thing, because the devil's process as they'd described it sounded like a lot of hard work for

105

almost no gain. But then I thought about my old throne in the backyard, and I understood something about the operator and the people she worked for, and I changed my question. "The devil," I said, and I just let the word hang for a minute in the air.

I thought she was going to yell at me or hang up, but she surprised me. "Sean," said Carol, the TBN telephone operator who was supposed to be taking down people's pledges, "praise the Lord, the devil has no dominion over us. He tries to take back the good things the Lord has done for us, but he can't, because that power isn't given into his dominion, amen?"

"The devil," I said, with a rising inflection to suggest more question coming, but then I found myself cupping my hand between my lips and the mouthpiece. I reached down into my imagination and made a strangled gurgling sound with my throat, vocalizing on the inhale and curling my tongue into various positions to make it sound like I was talking in reverse. I scared the hell out of myself with this sound: it felt real. I kept it up for the better part of a minute and a half.

Carol was a prayer warrior for Jesus working in Costa Mesa toward the end of the last age, and she was made of sturdier stuff than a young teenager might have guessed. "Devil," she said as soon as I was done, without any break to get her bearings, "you let go of Sean right now. He's heard the Good News tonight and nothing you can put in his head can drive it out. You loose this child of God from your chains. In the name of Jesus, I pray," she said. In my room a total silence took hold.

I said "Amen" the next time she asked for an *Amen*, but I was barely listening: I was lost in the story these people all believed, catching currents of it and riding them out into the far reaches of imagined possibility, believing everything they believed but from different angles, exciting perspectives, smoldering momentary vistas without end.

"Sean, you don't have to live as a slave," she said. "Jesus paid the price for you. Will you pray the sinner's prayer with me now?"

"I drink the blood of my slaves," I said, in a hushed-house whisper clean out of nowhere, shocking myself and feeling the power, and that was when she hung up.

Some lessons you learn gradually and some you learn in a sudden moment, like a flash going off in a dark room. I sift and rake and dig around in my vivid recollections of young Sean on the floor in summer, and I try to see what makes him tick, but I know a secret about young Sean, I guess, that he kind of ends up telling the world: nothing makes him tick. It just happens all by itself, *tick tick tick tick tick*, without any proximal cause, with nothing underneath it. He is like a jellyfish adrift in the sea, throbbing quietly in the warm waves of the surf just off the highway where the dusty white vans with smoked windows and indistinct decals near their wheel hubs roll innocently past.

I looked back over at the TV; everybody had their eyes firmly fixed on the guest, who was holding up more records by so many rock bands. He said the problem was everywhere, it was epidemic. But at that moment all I could see was the wolf in the white van, so alive, so strong. Hidden from view, unnoticed, concealed. And I thought, maybe he's real, this wolf, and he's really out there in a white van somewhere, riding around. Maybe he's in the far back, pacing back and forth, circling, the pads of his huge paws raw and cracking, his thick, sharp claws dully clicking against the raised rusty steel track ridges on the floor. Maybe he's sound asleep, or maybe he's just pretending. And then the van stops somewhere, maybe, and somebody gets out and walks around the side to the back and grabs hold of the handle and flings the doors open wide. Maybe whoever's kept him wears a mechanic's jumpsuit and some sunglasses, and he hasn't fed the great wolf for weeks, cruising the streets of the city at night, and the wolf's crazy with hunger now; he can't even think. Maybe he's not locked up in the back at all: he could be riding in the passenger seat, like a dog, just sitting and staring out the open window, looking around, checking everybody out. Maybe he's over in the other seat behind the steering wheel. Maybe he's *driving*.

I swept all the old medication bottles from the counter into a plastic bag, and I meant to throw them away, but I didn't want to. I didn't want to because . . . for a lot of reasons I didn't want to. As I put them into the bag one at a time I kept coming up with more reasons not to toss them out: casually, like I was trying out excuses. No reason seemed to hold its weight for long. I just couldn't throw the medications away, was the end of it. I tied a knot in the bag and I placed it back in the cabinet I'd been cleaning. I pushed it back a little ways, thinking to put it out of view, but then I thought better, and I looked at it for a minute before closing the cabinet. There was plenty more to clean. Old cleansers and rags by the dozen under the sink, canisters leaving rust rings on the contact paper. No shortage of things still left to do.

Two

11   I caught Vicky looking at my face in the light—I was sitting at my desk with some old pictures I'd dug out from an unmarked box. Me and my grandma running with geese somewhere. The zoo, I guess. Or on vacation. I wasn't sure.

If I'm in a bathroom out there in the world someplace I'll catch the glint myself on the raised ridges on either side of my mouth area, the dully shining skin. "Pretty bad?" I said.

"No, now, no," she said, with a little catching laugh in her breath. "You know I work doubles on weekends out at Loma Linda, though."

"No," I said. My conceptions of people's outside lives are pretty crude: basic, two-dimensional stuff.

"I do, I do," she said. "Anyway, my sister's friend works reconstructive. They had somebody like you in there just last week."

Our eyes met. This doesn't happen for me often, with any-body. It felt so naked. I tried to stay with it, to be present for it, to see where it would go.

"They can do so many things now, honey," she said, returning her eyes to her work. She was prepping some swabs for my cleaning. "It's a lot they can do since you first got hurt."

"I—I know. I talked to them about it a couple years back."

"How long ago was that?" she said, her gaze back on me, pretty steady. You forget how well people know you, when they know you.

I opened a drawer on the left side of my desk, the personal business side, which doesn't see a lot of traffic. I moved some stuff around and found a few brochures. One was even from Loma Linda. Imagine.

Vicky looked them over. "They're in their own building now," she said. "This one is from when they were still over in the main surgery building." The western desert gives way a little. Marsh gas? Some smell on the wind. DON FACE MASK. TRACE BACK. CONTINUE DUE EAST. DIG SHELTER.

"Anyway," she said, "you could call them," and she swabbed my cheeks with some glycerine on a compress, so gentle it barely stung at all.

"It's your grandmother," Dad said on the phone after we'd finished up our opening moves today. "Last night she—she died last night."

When you shoot yourself in the face with a Marlin 39A, one thing you don't think about is what your father will tell his mother when it becomes necessary to tell her something's happened. My grandfather on my father's side had been dead for over a decade; he had a heart attack one day in the supermarket. I'd overheard my dad explaining it to Mom after he

114

came home early from work. "The aisle was empty, it was early," he said. "He was lying there for—for a little while." I was twelve; they took me to the funeral at Oak Park and I stood quietly imagining what the screams would sound like if the coffin lid sprung open and something crawled out.

Grandma stayed on alone in the giant house where my dad and his brothers had grown up. When, eventually, the climb up the stairs got to be too much, she moved downstairs, and the second floor became an accidental museum commemorating the last day anybody'd lived there. I used to hide out up there when we'd visit and try to get lost in the dusty, abandoned feeling of a place where nothing ever happens.

What they told my grandmother after the accident was that I had been in a car accident and that everyone else in the vehicle had been killed. This was an important detail, because lots of people get into car accidents and come out basically OK. They break arms or they get concussions, and maybe they get brain damage and can't remember things like they used to. But they don't look markedly different, unless maybe their face hits the windshield and the car catches fire and everybody else inside gets burned to death. These were two of the details my father had asked me to memorize in case Grandma ever asked me about the accident and to mention if she did. "She's not going to ask you to talk about it, I know she won't," he said. "But in case she does."

One of the therapists I had to go to later on tried getting me to talk about why I was angry at my parents, and I'd say I didn't think I really was particularly angry at them except maybe at

115

my dad for making me lie to his mother. I only had one grandma left; it felt wrong to tell her stories. "Is there anything earlier?" she'd say then, and I'd shake my head no: the main thing is having to lie to my grandmother. "So if that's the main thing," she said, once, "what are some of the other things?"

It gets to the point where you almost want to make something up just to keep them happy, to keep from being the person who makes them feel like they're wasting their time. But I try to be honest always. It's important to me.

"There aren't really any other things," I said.

In the early days there hadn't been anybody my parents weren't going to sue. But they would have needed my cooperation to go after anybody besides the gun people, so that's who they settled on: the gun people. Most lawyers would have strung them along for a while, I think. But the one they did find, in the Yellow Pages, was a good guy, and he told them point blank that nobody was ever going to get a dime from the gun people. That was the end of that idea. He told them their legal money would be better spent on somebody to negotiate with insurance companies—somebody who knew that accidents happen, and that that's what insurance is really for, after all. *Accident*: this was the great gift, free and clear, that the Yellow Pages lawyer gave my parents when they called him. He did also say that they might have a case if they wanted to sue whoever'd originally sold my father the rifle, though.

The gun shop where my father'd bought it was on Mission Avenue, down between the drive-in and a used-tires place. It was a stand-alone cinder block building on a weedy asphalt lot. The shop's owner, Ray, was the man who'd sold it to him; Ray had served in the First World War with my grandfather. My father hadn't yet been old enough to walk on the day his own father had introduced him to his old army buddy Ray. Ray owned the building and lived in a small room off the office. At some point before I was born his wife died; he hadn't remarried, and when my parents talked about him—when Dad would say, at dinner, that he was thinking about going to see Ray this week—I got the feeling that some unnamed duty was being invoked. And so I knew, when Dad told me we were going to Ray's one morning, that my father had undertaken some kind of internal strategic shift in his approach to dealing with what was left of his only son. His rage was still fresh, but he must have begun to sense the slow beginnings of its ebb.

I remember feeling perilously light in my body. As though a sudden wind might lift me and carry me across the parking lot. I think now I'd be able to identify that feeling as fear, but at the time it was strictly physical: the heaviness of my head, which was with me most days, seemed ignorable. Though I couldn't yet walk without help, I felt as we cruised down Monte Vista like I might have been able to go a block or two. It made me think about the future, whose actuality was very slowly coming into view for me. The days ahead, the months and years. I was seventeen, so my sense of time was still necessarily limited, but the hospital ceiling had taught me a thing or two about it. I could see it from the window of the car: even when my view hit the vanishing point, I knew there was more beyond it.

It was warm out; when we got there Ray was set up in a folding chair in the parking lot, his back against the side of the building by the door, face tan and wrinkled, reading the *Penny-Saver*. He looked up as we got out of the car; saw my dad, saw me, looked back at my dad. "Well, William," he said, with an audible period at the end of the salutation. Then he looked at me.

"Well, Sean," he said.

"Hi, Ray," I said.

"I heard about all this," he said. He didn't point at my face; there was no need. He just looked up at me from his chair in the shade, patient like old people are patient. He wasn't nervous; I had developed a sense for nervousness like an animal's. It was a relief to have somebody who could look at me and not be nervous.

"Pretty dumb," I said. I wasn't sure if I really meant that, but it was a thing I was trying out; it seemed to make people feel more comfortable. He looked at me like a jeweler appraising a stone.

"Can't argue with you there, Sean," he said after a while. "I'm glad you didn't manage to . . ." He cut off where most people cut off, and took the breath they tend to take. "I wish you hadn't," he said.

"Sorry," I said.

My father hadn't said anything yet, but then he said, "Ray," and Ray got up from his chair: it was a greeting without formalities. They shook hands; Ray took a deep breath as their eyes met. Then he clapped my dad's right shoulder with his left hand twice, and we all walked out of the morning sun and into the small tan stucco one-room shop with the signs in the window that keep the light out.

In the Conan books I loved back then, history went Technicolor. Men's lives ended violently and with great consequence, again and again, in glory or squalor according to their fate, and no matter how many times the exact same scene played out, it was always a huge deal; any offense was grievous, all revenge total. Conan prowled Cimmeria, in constant uproar; all Cimmerian truces were false, any tranquil scene certain to open onto vistas of blood washing over the near memories of their antecedents. Cimmeria convulsed without rest. Even in still moments, intrigue waited like gathering fog at dusk.

Inside Ray's the evening light had suspended itself once before sunset a long time ago, and it was never going to change again. Dust collected and massed on the counter displays: old black combs glued on yellowed cardboard mounts, thick glass jars full of dead spent bullets, a fraying L-mounted card half-stuffed with quarters for the City of Hope. There was no future there; its past was a ghostless harbor. Nothing inside would ever leave the building.

I think Ray got that my father had come on some errand he couldn't really talk about, something he would have been embarrassed or ashamed to bring up. My father's errand was also partially or completely hidden from his own understanding, I think: he was improvising. Once we were inside they mainly talked grown-men talk, nothing talk: mutual friends; weather; the L.A. Rams. "Gone out to see—see the Rams yet?" my dad said, and Ray said, "No, not yet."

Eventually, like a wall-mounted camera sweeping the room,

Ray turned his attention my way. I was loitering near a fish-bowl filled with rifle casings, wanting to plunge my hand in up to my wrist, when he started in on a thing about how a gun's not a toy. My father, his friend—guys like Ray—they seemed to have so much trouble understanding even the most obvious things.

"A big part of being old enough to handle a weapon is re-specting its power," he said.

"I know, sir," I said. I called my father's friends *sir* reflex-ively. It was hard to remember they were real people sometimes.

"Well, I guess you do, now," said Ray, reaching for some point. But he didn't have a real sense of what he hoped to say; he was lost. As I became surer of this it felt like warm light gently flowing through me. It was hard not to smile.

"Yes, sir," I said.

Ray carried on for a minute about the power of guns, and the costs of not revering that power; after a while I stopped listening. I let the barren-void melody of his voice lilt its way through the inattentive chambers of my brain. The emotion rising in his voice, his ongoing efforts to control it: I had a brief fantasy of ratting my parents out, of explaining how they'd heard from a lawyer that Ray was the guy to go after if they were going to sue anybody and we were here to see how that idea felt with him right in front of us. But it would have hurt his feelings, and I couldn't stand it. I wanted to stop him, to explain to him that I had already known about guns when I walked down the hall from my bedroom to the living room while everybody was asleep; that I probably knew more about guns and bullets now than him or anybody he knew. But he would have taken it the wrong way, and I felt like he was probably enjoying himself. So I stood in a state of partial focus, waiting. Looking for an opening, and then not looking, because I wanted to let my dad and his friend do what they felt like they had to do here. I did hope that at some point I'd be able to explain my recent theory that it isn't really possible to kill yourself, that everybody goes on forever in multiple dimensions, which was less a theory than an attempt to do exactly what Ray'd been doing since he started talking: to draw some lesson from a place where no lessons were.

There was a poster on the wall behind the cash register; it was a poster I'd also seen in auto repair shops and maybe some other places, I couldn't remember exactly. It showed a bunch of little cartoon guys doubled over with laughter, their eyes shut from laughing so hard, their chubby little hands clutching their bellies. The caption underneath said: YOU WANT IT WHEN . . . ? I get the joke now, but then it was completely meaningless to me. It could have been in some foreign alphabet, except it wasn't: I understood all the words, but together, in that sequence, with that picture, to my mind, they were chaos. And so, in a different way, were Ray's musings, his helpful admonishments and his stern encouragements. They tried to reach across a divide whose distance he couldn't accurately gauge. But while the person I'd been just a few months before might have understood this and sneered, the person who'd emerged from his bandages saw the impasse and felt something soften inside. I wanted to put my hand on Ray's shoulder and tell him that when I said I was sorry earlier, I really meant it. But instead I nodded my heavy nod as he went on, and shook his hand before we left, and drew a few connections between things in my head as the car headed east again on Mission.

As you rappel down cascading chains of mutated ivy, you taste the air. It's different down here. The all-pervasive dust that clots your lungs begins to clear itself out in coughing spasms whose violence subsides as you descend. The smell of the ivy restores your hope in the journey. Your feet ache to touch fresh ground below.

The descent to the upper catwalk takes two hours, which are spent in a crisscrossing pattern among available vines. Your arms and ankles burn when you land; you tear off a handful of leaves when your feet hit the steel grating and stuff them into your mouth. They are moist and bitter. A new clarity gradually seizes your vision as you cast your gaze around and beneath.

You're inside a cylinder, a silo some thousand yards high; from your perch you can see that it continues down into the earth for many thousands more. It must have taken years to dig so deep. To build the broken network of platforms you must now navigate. To construct, from available scrap, sanded smooth and disinfected to keep the interior clean, the descending entryway to the kingdom beyond.

When I got home my mom asked me what Ray'd had to say. That was how she put it: "So, Sean, did you have a good day, what did Ray have to say?"

"He said guns are awesome," I said. It was a mean thing to say, and I was immediately sorry, but it was too late. My mother's shoulders stiffened, and she held her hand at her chin, two fingers pressed across her lips.

"Sean, you don't—" she said, and then she stopped to draw in some breath and try to keep her composure. "You don't understand," she said finally. Like most things she started to say about the accident, this went nowhere: there were too many places for it to go, so when it opened out onto its great vista of sad possibilities it just rested there, frozen by the view.

"I do, I do, Mom," I said. We were standing in the living room; Dad was in the bathroom. "Ray said I had to respect guns, is all, it was—"

I took my mother's hand between my hands. I felt like a very old man who had lived for a very long time; I knew I wasn't that old man, not really. I hadn't actually come into possession of any great wisdom, hadn't been on a quest that had seasoned me and invested my words and actions with meaning. But the sheen of it, the reflection maybe of a wisdom I might someday still attain, was visible to me for a second, and I felt the weight of what I'd done to them press against my chest like a heavy hand. "It was a funny thing for him to say, is all."

Mom wanted to meet me out there in the space I was trying to clear. But she couldn't do it, and I couldn't blame her then, and I don't now. There was too much wreckage in that space for her to stand.

My father came in then and saw Mom crying, and he was mad. He must have been mad already, after taking me down to Ray's with some uncertain hope in mind, looking for some conclusive moment and not getting it: I was pretty sure about this. Instead it had been another incident without clear lessons.

"Why do you have to make your mother sad?" he said in his louder voice, the one he saved for when he wanted to be heard. "Haven't you done enough—" he said, his stutter catching him at a crucial moment; I could see it make him even angrier. He kept his eyes firmly on mine. "Done enough already?" he said at last.

"It was an accident," I said, and Mom put a hand on his shoulder and said it was really OK, that there'd been a misunderstanding, and Dad's face did that thing it had recently learned to do: where his expression skidded across a sliding drift from anger to sadness to something else that didn't quite have a name, all in the course of a few seconds.

"OK, Sean," he said, "sorry, sorry to yell." We stood in our little triangle and then the doorbell rang; Dad had ordered some pizza for dinner. He put out some plates with a knife and fork by mine, and we all sat down to eat. Mom asked him the same question she'd asked me, in the same words—"What did Ray have to say?"—and Dad tried his best to explain why he hadn't really said much to Ray about liability and so forth, and Mom didn't say anything back, and then after a while Dad got up from the table and turned on the evening news with the volume too high.

Conan the Barbarian has no parents, as far as I know, but in my mind he was my model: trying to stand strong and brave, sword in hand, black hair flowing. In truth I have very little hair on my head now, and the hair I do have tends to clump in stringy clusters, but if my eyes are closed and my concentration is strong I can form a different picture of myself in my mind, so this was what I did, standing by the waist-high desk where the phone was. I closed my eyes and I concentrated. Dad was getting ready to tell me about the funeral plans, I knew. I could make it easier for him if I tried hard enough. It isn't really much of a mystery, this occasional need I have to comfort my father. I did something terrible to his son once.

"Grandma lived a long time," I said. Ten-plus years since Dad took me down to Ray's on that open-ended mission where nobody got revenge and nothing got resolved, and a whole lot of empty ground in the space from now to then. I have a theory that the less you say when someone dies, the better. Leave everything as open as you can.

"Thanks, Sean," he said. "For me this is hard, I—"

"Terrible," I said.

"No, no," he said, "that's—it's all really hard, but what I actually—I—"

"Not—"

"No, what—Sean, I don't like to say this; I know you loved your grandmother, and she loved you, but we—" Pausing here. Some things you practice a few times but it doesn't make them any easier. I could hear it now. "We don't think you should come to the funeral. I know that's—"

He just left it there for a second.

"It's really hard to—"

When anger rears up in me I have a trick I do where I picture it as a freshly uncoiled snake dropping down from the jungle canopy and heading for my neck. If I look at it directly it'll disappear, but I have to do it while the snake's still dropping or it will strike. This sounds like something they'd teach you in therapy at the hospital or something, but it's not. It's just a trick I found somewhere by myself. Once you've looked at a deadly thing and seen it disappear, what more is there to do? Walk on through the empty jungle toward the city past the clearing.

"It's OK, Dad," I said, evenly. I took stock of how I really felt: found all the various threads, saw which way they all ran. "Dad, it's OK. I get it. It's all right." And I do get it: I am not a welcome presence at a funeral, no matter whose it is. If I let myself stay mad about that I will go insane.

On the other end my father, now an orphan, was crying.

"Thank you, Sean," he said. "I don't mean to be awful to you. It's just—it's hard for me to ask, it's really hard. Your grandmother was so happy back in those early days, back when—"

The little silence that followed wasn't my dad's repetitive stutter. I could hear him entering a space he usually tried to avoid, finding himself on the other side of a door he wouldn't normally open. I followed him in.

"When you were a baby," he said, at last.

He sounded like he was choking. "It's OK, Dad," I said. "It'll be OK." CLAN SCARECROW, I saw penned in neat script on a little card inside my head.

12

I stood with the phone at my ear and tried to think of something to say. My father plays his cards close to his chest, but I felt like there was an opening here, a portal: a seam in the surface I was supposed to notice and pull open and climb through. That was why it was Dad calling, not Mom. So I took a quiet breath and put on my grown-up voice, the one I use when somebody looking for me gets ahold of my phone number.

"Dad, I'm sorry," I said. Nothing. "Hard to know . . ." I had no idea how to finish that thought.

"It is hard," he said. "Your grandmother . . . that was my mother."

It was a simple truth, something self-apparent. Something somebody might point out to you in kindergarten: when your dad was little, your grandmother was just his mom. Like looking at a 9 upside-down. I pictured my dad as a teenager: hair combed straight and parted on the side, head cocked at the direction of a portrait studio photographer. Big smile and a far-off gaze. "Dad, I am so, so sorry," I said, and I could see the distance from the rim of the tower to the ground, all that wasted Kansas plain going on and on forever, soaking up daylight and cooling to an inky black at night that spreads out uninterrupted for so long that eventually you can't see any tower at all.

I let people play for free in the early days. It was hard for me to imagine anybody signing up for a subscription without having gone through the first few passes, so I took out a dozen ads, some in bigger magazines, some in tiny self-published things I'd found at the comic store. The smaller ones sometimes didn't re-set my type: they'd just shrink it a little, and when it ran, it looked just like it had when I'd stuffed it into an envelope at my desk. NEW BY-MAIL GAME—DEADLY FUTURE/IRRADIATED WORLD. FIGHT TO SURVIVE IN SEARCH OF THE TRACE ITALIAN, my copy read. PLAY FOUR TURNS FREE. SEND FOUR SELF-ADDRESSED STAMPED ENVELOPES TO: FOCUS GAMES, BOX 750-F, MONTCLAIR CA 91762. The *F* stood for *The Magazine of Fantasy and Science Fiction*; if the ad ran in *Analog*, I'd use *A*. Somewhere I'd read that this was a way to keep track of which ads brought in more business, but that wasn't why I did it. I just thought there was something cool about using different box numbers for different places, something trivially arcane.

If you don't get drawn in by the free turns, you're not likely to keep playing, so I came up with the idea of putting players in classes, like when you're a kid outside playing and you're either a cop or a robber. But I didn't want there to be teams, because the problem with cops and robbers had always been that there was no scope to the action. It was basically just hide and seek; I wanted to be a robber who killed his victims, or the robber with X-ray eyes, or the one who could walk through walls and ends up in a special jail designed just for him. I wanted cops and robbers to last beyond the apprehension of the suspect. If we were playing cowboys and Indians all I could think about was how the actual point of the game was for one team to murder everybody on the other, and how the winners could be riding off covered in blood, which was how they'd look when they ran across somebody who hadn't been in the battle, and they'd have to explain themselves.

What I came up with for the Trace was elegant, I think, and simpler in function than it felt like in play. The first two turns led directly to a fork in the road, and that branched out onto three or four different paths. Three or four in my first, crudest pass: then six paths, then eight. As many as I could stand. The hub of the third turn would be an immense wheel, and you'd pick a spoke that would determine the course of the rest of your life. I saw stars when I thought about it. Usually when people stand at an intersection like the third turn hub they're not conscious of their position: they don't know where, in the course of their lives, they stand.

In the Trace you know. I made it clear in the text that this was a decisive moment, even in the original draft: You sense you're no longer alone in the old movie house, then you hear people knocking things over out in the lobby. On the floor you crawl through the dark, from your seat in the front row toward the glowing green EXIT sign. Bits of rotting carpet flake off beneath your fingernails. You're almost to the door down the hallway when you fall through the floor. ALL CLANS IN BIG WAYSTATION ROOM UNDERNEATH THE THEATER, I wrote excitedly in my sky-blue Mead notebook when I got the idea. ONE CLAN EACH CORNER, ONE MIDDLE OF ROOM, WARRIOR CLAN AT FURNACE?? These early drafts were always full of excited possibilities; they were written without outlines or diagrams, you can see them taking shape as they go.

You have to lie still until the militia leaves: you can hear them upstairs, sweeping the theater, knocking stuff over, pulling down drapes. You get a few pages describing the people around you down there in the basement: how they're dressed, whether they look friendly or smart or mean or well-armed or hungry. At the end of the turn, your choice is open: It is late and your eyes are heavy; you'll have to sleep here. Which group will you join?

At that point you have to boil down your decision to some descriptive term of your own choosing based on what you've read about the other people in the room, who've been sketched in groups—the ones crouched around a space heater, the ones hunched over an old road atlas. It works every time; I never have to explain. When a player writes back after the movie theater raid, I read what he says, and then I go to the files and I pick out a path. The total number of clans is infinite, but there are only sixteen paths, identified by Roman numerals, because people like the kid I used to be have always really liked Roman numerals. Beyond those are sixteen more I never assign, because they lead nowhere. They are unfinished, dead ends.

To the player, of course, the path is invisible. The point of the night spent underneath the theater for the player is to find out who he is. But the people he meets down there—the clan with which he becomes identified for the rest of his life in the game—will all be killed within a turn or two, or else he'll get

130

separated from them in the rail yard, or they'll all find the surface by daytime and eat cactus and go insane while the player, who wasn't hungry, has to watch. Something will happen. When it does, he's left with a name that he picked, a way of identifying himself. "I join the warlords," somebody will write in response to this turn, and then the next week, in an envelope he addressed to himself, he'll get a small card, like an old library card, on stiff mottled gray card stock: CLAN WAR- LORD, it will say in my weak imitation calligraphy. *All rights and privileges* in smaller script underneath.

I personally don't play. I can't. I wouldn't really want to, either, I guess. But I do have a card of my own, which sits in the front drawer of my desk. I'm clan seeker/digger. It's Path IV, the one that ends up sticking to the foothills along a semi- northward pass. The first player ever to head down it wrote in and said, *I go over to the seeker/diggers*: he meant the group with the army bags full of tools, the ones who'd comman- deered the film screen and were using it as a tarp. I wrote out a card that said CLAN SEEKER/DIGGER, but that didn't look right, so I made him up a new one that said SCOUT, and then I kept his original card for myself. I have to admit that I like and am pretty self-satisfied with my position as the only mem- ber of this sublimated clan. The one-man clan who exists only in rough draft. The player with a clan but no path. Scepter- wielding king of the class-A seeker/diggers.

In the metal drawers where the gears of the Trace are housed I keep a stray file that's really only there for motivation. It holds about a dozen pages, delinquent bits and pieces from lost time before their then-unknown predicate had been identified. I could pin everything inside it to a single corkboard and hang it on the wall near my desk; I feel like that's what most people would do. It's good knowing it's in the drawer, this one file, at arm's reach but hidden away in the dark back behind the more important things.

In it, among other things, is a list I made in the sixth grade, when I was twelve. We'd had a substitute teacher desperate to rein in the energy of the room for maybe fifteen minutes; after we came in from morning recess our desks were waiting for us with single sheets of blank lined paper on them and the words *Five Things You Want To Be When You Grow Up* written in colored chalk on the board, flowing cursive script three or four inches high, and *QUIET TIME* in big block capitals underneath. Everybody set to work; the sub strolled down the rows of desks where we sat writing in silence. As we finished we'd get up, one at a time, and put our pages in a basket on the desk, and when all of them had been handed in, she reached in and grabbed one from the pile.

It was mine, of course; she just picked it up and started reading it out loud in her deep, dusky substitute voice. She didn't say who it was by, or look in my direction while she read; I don't think she'd had enough time to connect names to faces in the half-day she'd been with us. But the blood rushed to my face all the same, and I remember my anger at hearing my real dreams spoken out loud by someone else's uncomprehending voice. "Number five, sonic hearing," she said. "Number four, marauder. Number three, power of flight. Number two, money lender. Number one, true vision." Some of the other kids shot laughing looks at one another. It was horrible.

People talk sometimes about standing up for what they believe in, but when I hear people talk like that, it seems like they might as well be talking about time travel, or shape-changing at will. I felt righteousness clotting in my throat, hot acid: the other kids were suppressing laughter and exchanging glances; the whole thing was so funny to them they had to punch their thighs to keep from cackling out loud. None of them had actually made a true list like mine, I thought, though this was conjecture. I wanted to defend my high stations, to tell them that what they were laughing at was something real, something vast. But no one was looking directly at me; everyone was looking around to see who'd flinch, and I picked up on this just in time to join them in scanning faces around the room, pretending to hunt for the list's author. And I kept my mouth shut, and then the sub said, "Here's another," and moved on to somebody else's list, which consisted of actual occupations, things you might really become out there in the world once you got out of school. They sounded like weak things compared with my list; I kept my thoughts to myself.

I remember this scene because it was embarrassing to live through it, and because remembering it is a way of knowing that I am half-true to my beliefs when the time comes. I sit silently defending them and I don't sell them out, but I put on a face that lets people think I'm on the winning team, that I'm laughing along with them instead of just standing among them. I save the best parts for myself and savor them in silence. Number three, power of flight. Number four, marauder. Enough vision to really see something. A stack of gold coins and a ledger. People want all kinds of things out of life, I knew early on. People with certain sorts of ambitions are safe in the Trace.

So while everybody else was at the funeral I was down at the Montclair Chamber of Commerce reinstating my business license. I'm supposed to renew it once a year, but the bills they send out don't look like much of anything so sometimes they get tossed out. When this happens I get new envelopes marked URGENT, and then I have to apply in person to have the license reinstated: renewal you can do by mail, but once they've put the license on hold you have to show up in person.

People look up from what they're doing when I enter a building. Famous people are probably quite used to this; I'm used to it, too, but sometimes, on good days, I feel like my job is to try to set them at ease. This I do by pretending everything is normal; the secret is to believe it in your heart, which comes more naturally than you'd think. So I meet their gazes gently, and I nod my head as lightly as I can, which is almost like executing a pirouette. I try to get them to find my eyes, which are still as they were on the day before the accident, and I try to hold them there as I pass. Unless they're being gauche about it: covering their mouths with their hands like somebody in an old horror movie, or whispering loudly to somebody nearby. Then I pop open my jaw as if I were trying to dislodge a stuck seed from my back teeth, and they get to see inside my mouth.

The window where you write the check to reinstate your business license is its own separate station at the end of a long fake-woodgrain counter where people come to pay less exotic bills: water bills, sewer bills. Business Licenses used to have its own separate room, but they had a big consolidation a few years back, and Business Licenses got moved in with the water and sewer people. I wouldn't care, but the people ahead of me in line always get nervous when they hear my breathing, which has a wet sound that I can't help.

I stood in my short line trying to keep my breathing even, and when I got to the front of it I strode purposefully down past the utilities windows toward my stop, and there wouldn't be anything else to say about the whole thing if my eye hadn't caught a nameplate atop one of the sewer-and-water tellers' windows as I passed: CHRIS HAYNES. The clerk behind it was young, with a weak goatee; there was no way it wasn't him. Even in passing you could see the younger man he'd once been, the oily grease on that young man's chubbier cheeks, the posters on his bedroom wall. He was helping a customer and he didn't see me, and I kept my pace steady and didn't make any gestures, but my heart leapt in my chest, and a few dark corners of my imagination were suddenly flooded with a cleansing light I knew was permanent.

There's an immense mosaic on the plaza, embedded in the concrete outside the doors of the Chamber of Commerce. It shows a man with a nose so long it must be a costume nose of some kind; he's holding a dish in his outstretched palm, while a person with a headdress, who could be a man or a woman, stands opposite him, reaching into the dish with finger and thumb together in a plucking gesture. From the first time I saw this I assumed it had something to do with a native local population I didn't know anything about. I loved that I didn't know, that there weren't any signs about it: the mosaic, too big and colorful to escape notice, tells no story to anyone and is seen by all. Maybe there's a plaque explaining it elsewhere on the plaza, but I've never seen it, so the mystery's intact.

As you leave the Chamber you have to walk across the mosaic; even if you're not looking down, its colors and shapes will bleed into your field of view. Back at the high school there used to be a superstition about an inlay in the concrete near the office, a multisided star: you weren't supposed to step on it or something bad would happen to you, I forget what. Bad luck. People would turn and walk around it, or rear up and take a big leap across when they got to it. You wondered if anybody actually believed in it, even one person. But everybody did it anyway.

Back home the mail had come. Two smart kids from the scavenger clan who'd cleared Tularosa a few turns before were plotting a course for Kansas. I consider it unethical to give anybody any help, and it's usually pretty easy to stay impartial, but I really wanted these two to make it; they were the most committed players to come along in quite some time, young and excited and full of jittery asides. *First night in Oklahoma and hopefully the last!* they started out this time. *We know we gotta keep going north we've got our sites on the barb wire!* which was a reference to something they'd read in one of the papers they'd taken from the fortune teller's body.

I sent them duly north, to a gas station near a reservation where they had to sleep because it was cold. Trace Italian was mostly written over the course of a year or two. I kept adding new turns for a while, injecting detours or increasing ellipses as the need arose: I saw a few patterns developing in live play and responded with byways that would extend the lead-up to a few payoffs. Once ranks began to thin, I almost never had to write new turns; the kinds of players whose letters warranted real action were usually the first to get distracted and quit. This turn was among the newer ones, the later ones. It was an empty turn, a turn where nothing happened, and that was because it had a ghost in it, and the ghost was Chris. His initials were suffocating there amid overlapping graffiti tags on the gas station walls. REZ LIFE. CATHY TORREZ. MIKEY T. CH. JESUS IS LORD. YOU SUCK. NAG WEST SIDE. 40 CREW. Chris Haynes. Chris the digger. Dead Chris, who'd seen the future and counted himself out.

13 It felt like so much was happening: I don't lead a busy life. The externals of the world I've built are quiet and even. Even small events amount to a shift in the current. All that movement and then Kimmy knocking out of nowhere, and me answering the door with my unwashed face, my hair all messy.

"You're still around!" she said in that one voice, the one from the other side of something. For a minute I was an astronaut having dreams about space: letting her voice register, feeling what it's like to be in the presence of somebody who isn't surprised by how I look.

"Still hanging around," I said back, opening the door a little more to let her in, and then she did come in, just like that.

By the window in the living room there's a soft chair that looks out onto the walkway. In Southern California even the most modest complexes keep their landscaping up; my walkway curves on its way out to the street. There's a sudden turn that takes you out around a small rounded hedge and some birds-of-paradise; my chair by the window is angled so that the corner of your eye catches this little flash of color and growth if you're gazing out toward the traffic or straight down at the dull grass.

Kimmy plopped herself down in the chair like a teenager visiting somebody's parents' house, and she cocked her head at me and said, "You look like shit," which was an old joke of ours, I'm pretty sure. It had that old joke feel. But I couldn't really latch on to the specifics of it, whether there was some rote response I was supposed to give back to show I remembered. But I didn't, so I just stood there, dumb and big, looking at her, trying to figure out how I felt.

You hear a rumbling in the Texas dust. Clouds form in the dirt. They lift and join together until it's just dusty air everywhere, brown and dirty. You could run, but you can't see more than a foot or two ahead at a time, and you're coughing. You bury your face in the crook of your arm and breathe in through your sleeve.

Your first guess is that this is an earthquake, but as the minutes pass and the rumbling grows louder you remember small quakes you used to feel in California. How long did those last? A minute at most. Never longer. And then the aftershocks. Now, beneath your feet, you feel the ground rising. There's no other way to think of it. The ground is rising.

You scramble back and you end up on all fours, watching as the earth cracks, like there's a giant underneath it pushing up against the lower surface with his fingers, about to break free. And then a structure punches up through the dry earth, crown first, sharp steel. But the map indicates that you are still far from the mark. Could the map be wrong? No: as the tower rises you see symbols that bear no resemblance to the ones you know will mark the spires of the Trace Italian. Half-scratched pictures, shapes that could be letters, clusters that could be numbers. This is not the bulwark, not the housing that guards the Trace. And still it rises.

Technically this move exists, but I have never sent it to anyone. I wrote it when I was eighteen. At my best I figure I'm only an OK writer; any good effects I have are things I got from people who are only considered good writers by young men who need to escape. I have my moments. But this move is made of cruder stuff; it was typed directly onto the page that became the master copy and I never revised it. I just put it in, and every time I get a chance to let somebody see it, I don't. Sometimes I wonder if people suspect they've been sent the substitute move, the one for players who pick "Move East" instead of "Treat Wounds" when they get to the way station that should lead here. Whether they get a feeling, something that tells them that where they are is a stand-in for the place they're supposed to be. Whether they suspect something. They almost never tell me if they do.

> *I did the math and also we keep a map. This is wrong*
> *there ought to be something else here. There was trail of*
> *mutant bodies they didn't just die of old age. It's cool*
> *I'll figure it out though. Our next move is to gather*
> *bones. We put them in our night packs. Gather bones.*
> *Well take it sleezy*
> *Lance*

The only one of my close friends I remember coming to see me in the hospital was Kimmy. I didn't have a whole lot of friends anyway, so I didn't feel abandoned so much as re-minded. A few people sent me letters: Joe from sixth-period U.S. history wrote, kind of from nowhere, to say he'd heard about what happened and was sorry; Barry, an old friend from grade school, wrote and said he hoped I was going to live, and he said it twice in the same letter, which kind of shook me up. Teague sent word somehow, through which channel I forget, and said he'd find me when the commotion died down, which I respected. He was a known presence. Showing up at my bed-side in his denim and feathered hair would only have made things more tense on balance.

But Kimmy started coming within a day or two after the nurses loosened up the visiting hours, and she came early and she stayed late. She strained to make out the constituent parts of the words I'd try to form and she'd help me arrange them into thoughts; she helped me find the path back to my self. This was why, later on, I enshrined her in a special place no one will ever see, which is kind of a shame, except that I did it on purpose, so it's only a shame if you limit yourself to the smaller picture.

It was a blank day about two weeks in. I didn't see her come through the door. My peripherals were shot, and my ears hummed like generators, so unless you were standing directly in front of me, leaning over me, I'd have no way of knowing you'd arrived. In stray moments above the surface, I'd some-times wonder if there were people at the head of the bed, standing there silently, waiting to see if I'd respond to the pres-ence of other people in the room. I'd say something from time to time just to check: "Hey?" or "Are you there?" This is differ-ent from calling out into a cave or well; it's a form of prayer.

She put her hand directly on my wrist. For those first few seconds of contact I had no idea who she was, and maybe that was why things panned out the way they did: from the dead depths of the infinite ceiling, a strange hand reached out and landed on my wrist, and rested there, warm and soft, and I felt so grateful for it. I drank in the simplicity of it, the soothing totality. Then Kimmy's head came craning into view. The only other people who touched me during those days were people who were being paid to do so; there was no feeling in their touch.

"Sean, you dumb shit," she said. She was crying but she kept her hand where it was. "What the fuck."

I was full of painkillers; I could barely form single words without considerable effort. But I dug down deep and said, "Kimmy," while she stroked my wrist.

"What did you do, what did you do," she said.

"I, hhuggh," I said. The dried blood in what was left of my oral cavity was coming loose, little bits of gummy candy lodged in my throat.

"Sean, you dumb shit, you stupid asshole," she said. The close air of the room framed her words in such a way that their specific weight, their breathy heft, has never left me.

"I, hnnuggh," I said, and with great effort used my neck and shoulders to move my head enough to see her where she stood, leaning there, seeing all of me and looking ready to see more if she had to. For reasons that seem obvious to me, I don't believe in happy endings or even in endings at all, but I am as susceptible to moments of indulgent fantasy as anybody else. When I picture the scene just then, when I remember it

142

right, I imagine a story where Kimmy and I grow up and get married. To each other.

> *pass through crystal gate*
> *cut central cables*
> *food, water, gauze*
> *sewn patches for light uniform*

I spent a few minutes in deep concentration trying to decide what I thought about this: it was the opening four-line salvo of a two-page letter from Chris, and it continued on in this way jaggedly toward its inevitable terminating *CH*.

> *invert map*
> *Hansel and Gretel*
> *ration supplies*
> *defogger*
> *knife*

It was a mixture of styles: the imperative chosen from the list of available options, the tell-your-own-story tendency that most players settle happily into, the wild compression that made Chris so strange and special. But it was lost in itself here; I didn't know what he was talking about.

> *mark signposts if any*
> *flora/fauna*
> *hydrate*

circular detours when possible
gloves
bedding
protective glasses

Nobody has any protective glasses; they're not something I would have thought to include in the game. Nobody needs to hydrate: the movement of the game is simpler than all that. Detours? Those come from my side of the table, not the player's. I guessed that the second page might contain some one-line summation of what I'd been reading; I thought maybe Chris was fleshing out his experience and letting me in on the process. Instead it continued in the same way:

call mom?
blade
bat
memorize passwords
flint and gel fuel
saline mist
"focus"
check map inversion at intervals
rest in open
love enemies/friends
note tacked to near post
when tower in view.

Saline mist? Gel fuel? Crystal gate? These were touchpoints from somebody else's dream, traces of the fallout from somebody else's accident. I pulled REST AND RESTORE from the actual options that Chris had been offered at the end of his last turn. REST AND RESTORE was a placekeeper move of the sort you got every four moves or so; they drew out your time and imparted a sense of depth without moving your play ahead too fast. I knew that some people who'd get that would instinctively take advantage of these moves if they needed to. People don't play games like mine with a view toward not having anything left to play.

My dad came straight to the hospital from work. When he got here Kimmy was sitting bedside on one of the three-legged rolling stools with the circular seats that doctors use. She was pushing herself back and forth, half a foot this way, half a foot back, rocking. "What have we here?" said my dad, which was something he always said: most of the time it more or less just meant "Hello," but it was an actual question here.

"Mr. Phillips," said Kimmy, and she got up to hug him, which was a thing she did to absolutely everybody; it was one of the things I liked about her. But my father left his arms at his sides, leaving Kimmy to squeeze his ribs like a person on angel dust hugging a stop sign. They remained that way for a few seconds; I could only make out the edges of the scene but it made me squirm.

"What do you know about this?" my father said when she'd let him go.

"What do I know?"

"What do you know?" my dad said.

"Probably as much as you know." She was a little angry now. I could hear it. It was kind of exciting; people were pretty selective about how they let themselves feel when they were in my room.

"That's probably not—probably not true," said my dad. "We don't know anything at all, his mother and me, we don't know anything."

I moaned in protest. Kimmy's fingers brushed my hand, hanging down by the siderail.

"I don't either!" she said, and then: "What are you even talking about?"

As Dad answered I could hear in his voice that he'd been rehearsing these lines, getting them ready. Sometimes I'd catch him at the mirror in the morning while he shaved, testing out things he might later say to his boss or to his friends at work. When he's heading toward some specific point, you can't miss it: it's in the air. All my life this has given me the creeps.

"We called your parents," he said. I wished I could see her face from where I lay, wished I could see the response in her eyes. "We think somebody knew something about this. About all this. Before."

"Before?" she said. I loved her anger, how much she resented my father just then. "I don't—"

"Well," he said, "we think you probably do." When I imagine this scene as part of a movie, the minute of silence after my father says this is extended for an hour or so, and then the credits roll.

At the northern gate of Camp Oklahoma the capos have gathered around a pit fire. It is late at night and the stars above you

shine, huge oceans of milky light. Too dehydrated to stand up, you
hunker forward on your knees and elbows, prepared to fight with
your fists and your teeth if it comes to that. An outcropping of
sage provides partial cover, but if you stand up you will be seen.

Around the fire stand the guards, consulting either a map or
some blueprints, it's hard to tell. In Camp Oklahoma you are
adrift, and each turn you take could be the one that leads you back
to the same crag wall you landed against when you jumped off the
train. No matter how many possible plans of the compound you
sketch out in the dirt beneath you, none of them seem accurate,
and your days and their stops have begun to blur in your mind.
Beyond the soldiers stands the gate, locked but maybe scalable, pos-
sibly electrified. The unlabeled bottle of pills that remains from
your pharmacy run three days ago presses into your thigh through
your pocket as the thirst turns your throat dry. Maybe you can make
some kind of a deal. Or maybe you'll just run straight for the fence.

I must have drifted off into dreamworld somewhere, which
would have made me feel ashamed if it hadn't been something
that happened all the time; I couldn't control whether I stayed
conscious or not just yet. "Sean, are you awake?" my father
said when the time came for him to make his move.

"Yeah," I said. I wouldn't be getting speech therapy
until after I'd been sent home; it took me ages to get to full
sentences.

"Sean," he said. I hate it when people say my name again
and again, like I'm going to forget who they're talking to. Over
the years I've developed a theory that the sicker you look, the
more people say your name. "Your mother and I want to talk
to you about Kimmy."

147

"Here?" I said; it sounded like I was asking if we might have this conversation somewhere else. But my father understood me. I wanted to know if Kimmy was here, if she'd come with them, if she was OK.

"No, no, Sean," said my dad. "We asked her parents to ask her not to come today. We want . . . we want to know why she keeps visiting you."

"Friends a long time," I said very carefully, very slowly, holding my spasming jaw as still as I could. I wanted to get the *r* in *friend* right, but I couldn't, so I said *fend*. Who knows what *long* even came out like.

"Yes, we know," he said. There was no mistaking his tone. "But we don't think she's been entirely honest with us."

I had been waiting for this. It was almost a relief. They'd been working variants of this line from the moment I'd first regained consciousness: "Who gave you this idea?" Things like that. I had very concrete fantasy scenarios in which I taught myself to speak again, clearly and coherently, with the explicit purpose of then being able to say to my parents *I don't know why I did it, it just happened, OK.* I didn't know yet how fantastic a scenario that was: to be able to look at someone whose need for reason and order has become truly desperate beyond all measure and tell them that it doesn't matter how cold it gets at night, they're just going to have to keep digging.

"Has," I said.

"I know you both say that, Sean," he said.

I was still heavily medicated, and when I had to infer something, to take a few details into account and form from them a conclusion, it happened in slow motion, with great deliberation. I saw my dad getting ready to say another thing he'd been preparing to say, some other part of the script, and I began to sense the scale of it: that he'd told himself a story and shared it with Mom, who'd written her own version of the same story, and then they'd compared versions until they'd arrived at one they could both believe in. It was my father's job now to make me tell them their story was true.

"We know," he went on, "that that's your story. But we think we have a pretty clear picture of what actually happened, and anyway, Kimmy didn't even try to live up to her end of the deal, so I really don't get how you can expect—" I could hear his anger, trying to work out a plot point he couldn't make fit.

"It doesn't matter," he said finally. "What does matter is that your mother and I . . ." And that was the point where I started to tune him out. When I try to recover his exact words from memory, I can only come up with composites, things that sound sewn together, unstable mixtures of what they'd de-cided to believe and what they couldn't figure out, and prob-ably some other stuff support services were telling them down on the second floor. I know the thrust of what he said involved their theory of a suicide pact, a theory that, in later years, made me feel great pity and shame: that they'd been driven to tell themselves this particular story, to settle for that—for something completely made up, an invention landed on by parents who'd found themselves in a terrible place quickly piecing together some ad-hoc narrative from random chunks of available data: comic books, movie posters, records and tapes. Sketches in my notebooks. Old toys. Things from the near side of an unbridgeable gulf. But the exact details of what he said are lost to me. When he was done, I said: "Totally wrong," which came out so bluntly that it made me laugh, which made him angrier.

He stood up and stayed there for a minute, silent, and then he left, and I thought about what it meant to still be alive, and then huge walls of earth began rising in formation inside me, spewing clouds of dust as they rose, right angles like dominos leaning against one another but refusing to fall, six or seven layers of ground beneath each rail buckling until they hit bedrock with a long, rolling, decisive thud, a chain reaction rippling out with great percussive power, the mud walls banding together for miles into a structure gigantic enough to be seen from space, a star-shaped beacon in the gray distance.

People bring you books, cheap paperbacks, when you're in the hospital: this was how I found out that I hate mystery novels. I tried Ellery Queen and Nero Wolfe. They just made me nervous. My parents wouldn't bring me my own books; they'd thrown most of my stuff away. So Kimmy brought me magazines to read. She'd sit bedside and flip through *Hit Parader* or *Circus* with me, and she brought some Robert E. Howard from the library, short stories. August Derleth. L. Sprague de Camp. Things she knew I liked.

"Mötley Crüe just got back from their tour of Japan," she'd say. "They look like dicks. Here." And then she'd hold the magazine up for me to see, and I'd laugh, and she'd say: "What are you laughing at, you look like a dickhead, too." But she never asked me why I'd done it, and I've wondered my whole life whether that was because she understood instinctively that it was a stupid question to ask, or because she thought maybe she understood something other people didn't.

I never found out whether my parents called hers and told them to keep their daughter away from me. There wasn't a traceable moment. But her visits became less frequent, and then she was gone. I would think about it sometimes, by myself, in empty hours. What happened? Nothing happened; Kimmy visited until she didn't feel like coming anymore, and then she stopped. I could be sad about it but I couldn't get angry, because I couldn't imagine being in her shoes and doing anything different. She told me, one of the last times I saw her, that she expected me to "get better," and this made her unique among all my visitors; my family didn't talk that way. They talked about me "coming home," or "getting out," but not getting better. Kimmy told me that I was going to get better. And she asked me whether I was going to do anything when I got out. "Are you going to do something when you get out?" That was how she put it. I said what teenage boys say about their plans: "I don't know."

Some things stick with you, great visions, and other things you never seem to learn: every few years I try to read a mystery novel or two, because they're always there in their hundreds at the Book Exchange, constituting the greatest part of the inventory. I see them and I remember trying to learn to like them in the hospital, and so I buy two at fifty cents apiece and try again. Ngaio Marsh. Ruth Rendell. I can't stand them, but I keep on trying. Are you going to do something when you get out? For all I knew she meant I should get out and finish the job I started; it's a possibility. But I took her to mean something else, and I held on to the idea as tightly as I could, focusing on it like a fixed point you stare at when trying to distract yourself from great physical pain.

Kimmy and her husband were out looking at houses. She was reading the street names out loud when she realized she was in my neighborhood. The husband was a guy she'd met at community college after high school. Paul. Nobody I knew.

"Where is he?" I asked.

"I had him drop me off," she said. "Meeting you would be kind of intense for him." She sounded, for just that moment, exactly as she had on the last day I'd seen her. But as we sat and talked, I could hear how she was a different person now. The change must have come gradually; an easy shift into adulthood, a softening. She told me about Paul's job—he was a regional manager for Enterprise—and how they didn't have any kids.

"Me neither," I said, and she laughed, but I saw her eyes: something more going on in there. But it flickered only once, and then she snapped back to the present.

We didn't visit long. She told me about her job, and her plans: ideas she had about opening a business, places she and Paul might move to so he could be closer to his work. She asked if I still knew anybody, and I said no, but I told her about Victory, how you get close to the people who take care of you in a weird way. I wanted to thank her for how she alone among all my friends had never let me see how sick the sight of my bandaged head must have made her feel, and I wanted to tell her I was sorry for any trouble I'd caused her back then, but I felt like it might spoil the mood, whose easy gravity seemed worth preserving. But I ended up breaking the spell anyway when I asked about JJ.

"JJ's dead," she said. There are so many different kinds of ghosts.

"What—"

"He got into drugs," she said. "Somebody shot him. That was, like, ten years ago." I started doing math in my head.

"Nobody really knew him anymore," she said. She took my hand in hers and gave it a squeeze like she used to do at the hospital. "We just kind of all did whatever after graduation."

Later, talking to Mom on the phone, I mentioned how Kimmy'd come around to visit. Mom tried not to sound irritated. "What did she want?" she asked.

"Nothing," I said.

"Really," said Mom.

"Just saying hi," I said. I knew ahead of time that Mom wasn't going to accept this answer, because she couldn't understand it, but I tried it out anyway. "She was in the neighborhood," I offered, hoping to hit the right tone so we wouldn't get into an argument, but I did not succeed.

14

"What do you have in this bottom drawer, now, that I can't open it and tidy it up a little?" Vicky said once. The bottom drawer is locked.

"Nothing I'm ever going to use," I said.

"You should let me just clean the whole cabinet, honey," she said.

"There's really no need," I said.

```
ARIZONA-NEW MEXICO-TEXAS-OKLAHOMA-KANSAS
NEVADA-UTAH-COLORADO-KANSAS
OREGON-IDAHO-WYOMING-UTAH-KANSAS
OREGON-IDAHO-WYOMING-COLORADO-KANSAS
ARIZONA-UTAH-COLORADO-KANSAS
ARIZONA-NEW MEXICO-COLORADO-KANSAS
ARIZONA-NEW MEXICO-OKLAHOMA PANHANDLE ONLY-
    KANSAS
OREGON-WASHINGTON-NORTHERN IDAHO-MONTANA-
    NORTH DAKOTA-SOUTH DAKOTA-NEBRASKA-KANSAS
```

OREGON-WASHINGTON-NORTHERN IDAHO-WYOMING-
   NEBRASKA-KANSAS

ARIZONA-UTAH-IDAHO-WYOMING-NEBRASKA-IOWA-
   MISSOURI-KANSAS

NEVADA-UTAH-COLORADO-KANSAS-MISSOURI-KANSAS

NEVADA-UTAH-COLORADO-KANSAS-NEBRASKA-KANSAS

ARIZONA-NEW MEXICO-TEXAS-OKLAHOMA PANHANDLE
   ONLY-COLORADO-NEBRASKA-KANSAS

ARIZONA-NEW MEXICO-TEXAS-TUNNEL UNDER
   OKLAHOMA-KANSAS

NEVADA-UTAH-COLORADO-NEW MEXICO-TUNNEL UNDER
   PANHANDLE-KANSAS

NEVADA-UTAH-COLORADO-NEBRASKA BORDER TUNNEL-
   KANSAS

ARIZONA-NEW MEXICO-TEXAS-LOUISIANA-
   MISSISSIPPI-ARKANSAS-MISSOURI-KANSAS

ARIZONA-NEW MEXICO-TEXAS-LOUISIANA-
   MISSISSIPPI-TENNESSEE-KENTUCKY-MISSOURI-
   KANSAS

ARIZONA-NEW MEXICO-TEXAS-LOUISIANA-
   MISSISSIPPI-TENNESSEE-KENTUCKY-INDIANA-
   ILLINOIS NO CHICAGO-IOWA-NEBRASKA-KANSAS

ARIZONA-NEW MEXICO-TEXAS-LOUISIANA-
   MISSISSIPPI-TENNESSEE-KENTUCKY-INDIANA-
   ILLINOIS (CHICAGO)-IOWA-NEBRASKA-KANSAS

NEVADA-UTAH-COLORADO-WYOMING-SOUTH DAKOTA-
   MINNESOTA-IOWA-NEBRASKA-KANSAS

NEVADA-UTAH-COLORADO-WYOMING-SOUTH DAKOTA-
   MINNESOTA-IOWA-MISSOURI-KANSAS

NEVADA–UTAH–COLORADO–WYOMING–SOUTH DAKOTA–
   MINNESOTA–IOWA–MISSOURI–ARKANSAS–OKLAHOMA–
   KANSAS

ARIZONA–NEW MEXICO–COLORADO–UTAH–WYOMING–
   NEBRASKA–KANSAS

OREGON–NEVADA–IDAHO–UTAH–COLORADO–KANSAS

OREGON–IDAHO–NEVADA–UTAH–COLORADO–KANSAS

OREGON–IDAHO–NEVADA–UTAH–COLORADO–PANHANDLE
   TUNNEL–KANSAS

OREGON DEAD END

ARIZONA DEAD END

BAJA CALIFORNIA–ARIZONA–NEW MEXICO–TEXAS–
   OKLAHOMA–KANSAS

BAJA CALIFORNIA–ARIZONA–SONORA–NEW MEXICO–
   TEXAS–OKLAHOMA–KANSAS

ARIZONA–SONORA–CHIHUAHUA–TEXAS–OKLAHOMA–
   KANSAS

NEVADA–CALIFORNIA–BAJA CALIFORNIA–ARIZONA–NEW
   MEXICO–TEXAS–OKLAHOMA–KANSAS

ARIZONA–CALIFORNIA–NEVADA–CALIFORNIA RETURN–
   ARIZONA–NEW MEXICO–SONORA–CHIHUAHUA–
   COAHUILA–TEXAS–OKLAHOMA–KANSAS

ARIZONA–NEW MEXICO–TEXAS–COAHUILA–TEXAS–
   OKLAHOMA–KANSAS

BAJA CALIFORNIA–SONORA–CHIHUAHUA–COAHUILA–
   TEXAS–OKLAHOMA–KANSAS

BAJA CALIFORNIA–SONORA–CHIHUAHUA–COAHUILA–
   TEXAS–OKLAHOMA DEAD END

BAJA CALIFORNIA–SONORA–CHIHUAHUA–COAHUILA–
   TEXAS DEAD END

```
BAJA CALIFORNIA-CALIFORNIA-BAJA RETURN-DEAD
   END
CALIFORNIA DEAD END
NEVADA-OREGON-WASHINGTON-OREGON-NEVADA-UTAH-
   COLORADO-KANSAS
NEVADA DEAD END
```

It's almost impossible to remember the fury of assembly, that time back home when the house was a way station: when I was unwelcome there and knew it; when I was a dark presence in other people's nearby lives, a person who made the house harder to live in. But the Trace had come home with me in bits and pieces: on Pomona Valley Hospital letterhead stationery, and in remembered scenes and phrases, fresh and vital. I wanted to make good on it before anything happened, before I got worse. Maybe I wouldn't get worse: it was hard to predict. *Hard to predict* was another thing I'd brought home from the hospital, a phrase that had become a secret personal talisman, something I didn't dwell on but kept nearby. I had headaches, and a pulsating ring that throbbed in my ears. I was still too weak to bear much weight. But I'd had an idle little dream in a small dead space, and the dream was now alive and hungry inside me.

It's really just simple math, the whole of it. There are only two stories: either you go forward or you die. But it's very hard to die, because all the turns pointing that way open up onto new ones, and you have to make the wrong choice enough times to really mean it. You have to stay focused. Very few players train their focus on death. The path forward stops here and there as you go, each frame filled out by outlines and figures from the rich depths of my hospital ceiling, shaded by colors I'd reconstituted from the foggy memory of the visions that had preceded the event for sixteen years: all those blurred plains, now melted down into an ideally endless landscape, its key peaks judiciously spread out so as not to use them all up at once. Saving some for last when there was no last. When there was no point in saving, when no one would ever see the very last.

I listened to music to drown out the drone, and I sat in my wheelchair exercising my legs so they'd be able to carry me when I left. I noticed how the blue padding on the seat of the chair retained heat, which made my thighs get sweaty and then clammy as I sat in it all day. I learned to hate it, and to look forward to the slow, hard work of physical therapy. Pain woke me up several times a night, as it would continue to do for over a year and, occasionally, forever, and I taught myself to power through it on the way back to sleep, because getting medication in the middle of the night was too sad and horrible to be worth it. I closed my eyes and pictured the stronghold I'd built as it would really look out there in the physical world, in the unknown Kansan expanse: it was vivid, and beautiful if you managed to get inside it. From without, it was stark, wind-swept, a silo in the middle of nowhere, nearly nothing in the middle of more nothing.

I filled notebook after notebook after notebook with para-graphs describing it, indicating its parameters, the directions leading to it or away from it, the coordinates of its hidden refuge. I annotated every page with numbers and abbreviations and self-invented legends that were hard to keep track of—which needed, eventually, a smaller notepad of their own—and some ideas that didn't fit but still seemed cool got ported off to new notebooks, where they grew into their own games, smaller concerns, exclusive worlds for players with specific needs. Little private exorcisms that would eventually find people in need of their hidden formulas. Barbarian Zone. Crosshairs. Wolf Patrol. It was like shrapnel scattering this way and that, who knows where it lands, but I kept my sites trained on Kansas; and I told my parents at dinner one night that I didn't need the TV in my room anymore, that they should sell it, and Dad said, "Really? Why?" because he knew I'd been watching lots of TV late at night for a while.

"Just don't need it," I said.

"Everything all right?" Dad said after he'd exchanged a look with Mom.

"Just too busy for TV," I said, trying to telegraph a smile with my tone of voice, in a small nod of my head, and everybody caught the same good mood for once, a rare grace for us in those days, the sort of high note that inspired dangerous, inexplicable thoughts in me, which I kept to myself until I could get back to work.

```
BYPASS-HUSK OF SEMI-BRUSH-HIGHWAY-OFF-RAMP
BYPASS-BRUSH-HUSK OF SEMI-HUSK DEFENSE-BRUSH
   CLEAR-OFF-RAMP
BYPASS-MASK DROP-BRUSH-CAUGHT-GARAGE
BYPASS-MASK DROP-BRUSH-CAUGHT-COMBAT-GARAGE
```

```
GARAGE-DECOY-MAIN STREET-POST OFFICE
GARAGE-DECOY-MAIN STREET-MARKET
GARAGE-COMBAT-CAUGHT-GARAGE
GARAGE-COMBAT-CAUGHT-OFFSITE
```

OFFSITE-SOLITARY

```
ACTION 1-REASON
ACTION 2-DECEPTION
ACTION 3-MADMAN
ACTION 4-DIGGING
```

OFFSITE-CELLMATE-ITEM EXCHANGE

```
ITEM EXCHANGE 1-AMMUNITION-MAP SKETCH
ITEM EXCHANGE 2-AMMUNITION-RATIONS
ITEM EXCHANGE 3-SECONDHAND MAP SKETCH-
   RATIONS
ITEM EXCHANGE 4-SECONDHAND MAP SKETCH-MAP
   SKETCH
ITEM EXCHANGE 5-MASK-MAP SKETCH
ITEM EXCHANGE 6-MASK-RATIONS
ITEM EXCHANGE 7-MASK-INFORMATION
ITEM EXCHANGE 8-SECONDHAND MAP SKETCH-
   INFORMATION
```

OFFSITE-CELLMATE-COMBAT

```
SEIZE ALL ITEMS
NO INFORMATION
```

I think about lizards that puff out their necks, or those brightly colored frogs down in the Amazon, coated with neurotoxins, adapting to their surroundings, their needs. But my head's not an evolutionary adaptation, so that's not quite right. All my reshaped parts seem like they protrude now, or hang; it can't be possible, I figure, but maybe they do, I haven't measured. Everything looks bigger to me in the mirror now. And when people out in the world see me, something in their expressions reminds me of people looking up at buildings. Sometimes I sit by the window, but the chair by the window feels almost like a platform. The window frames my face in such a way that my head seems monstrously huge.

Still, I make a point of working there sometimes, even though, as I say, there isn't so much work to do anymore. I thought about inventing a new game, but the Sean who built the Trace is as distant from me now as the Sean who blew his face off is from both of us. All three live in me, I guess, but those two, and God knows how many others, are like fading scents. I know they're still there. I could find them if I needed them. But I don't need them, and one of them survives only in bits and pieces. They certainly don't need me. They are complete just as they are.

It's one small thing I remember noticing in those months of building and making and drafting and plotting, something that seems less small over time: for a player to make progress, he has to pacify or destroy whoever's in his way. Those people become part of his story: he can't go back and breathe life into them, and whatever gains he gets from the wrecks he leaves behind are permanent in the sense that any other courses open to him beforehand will then become closed. So when I sketched the scene where a player, having been caught by warlord resource-hoarders and imprisoned in an improvised jail, could just kill his cellmate and get everything he might otherwise have spent six turns gathering, I didn't feel right about it: it was directly rewarding a player for attacking somebody who hadn't done him any harm, for doing the wrong thing. It saved the player all the work while giving him all the spoils. But I saw the bigger picture: that it was true. That to the player who intended to make it to safety, no one in front of him amounted to more than some stray marks on paper, half-real figures to be tunneled under or blasted through as you headed on east toward the spires.

```
VOORHEES-HUGOTON-ZIONVILLE-SURPRISE-KEARNEY-
    EMORY-WASHBURN-CORONADO
VOORHEES-VALPARAISO-IVANHOE-GARDEN CITY-
    LAKIN-KNAUSTON-MODOC-CORONADO
SHARON SPRINGS-EAGLE TAIL-HACKBERRY CREEK-
    SCOTT CITY-CORONADO
BLAIR-HURON-HORTON-WHITING-TRAIN TO TOPEKA-
    TRAIN TO KANAPOLIS-LYONS-GREAT BEND-NESS
    CITY-DIGHTON-SCOTT CITY-CORONADO
MANHATTAN-SALINA-KANAPOLIS-LYONS-GREAT
    BEND-NESS CITY-DIGHTON-SCOTT CITY-
    CORONADO
BIRD CITY-SHERMANVILLE-EUSTIS-EAGLE TAIL-
    SHARON SPRINGS-TRIBUNE-CORONADO
MONTERO-HECTOR-TRIBUNE-CORONADO
KANORADO-HORACE-LEOTA-CORONADO
COOLIDGE-CARLISLE-EMORY-FEDERAL-WASHBURN-
    CORONADO
```

```
JETMORE-PAWNEE VALLEY-PETERSBURG-SCOTT CITY-
    CORONADO
RICHFIELD-LAPORTE-EMORY-WASHBURN-CORONADO
RICHFIELD-DERMOT-ZIONVILLE-EMORY-WASHBURN-
    CORONADO
SHIELDS-CHEYENNE TOWNSHIP-SCOTT CITY-MODOC-
    CORONADO
CUTTS-ELLEN-SCOTT CITY-MODOC-CORONADO
ATWOOD-RAWLINS-COLBY-BOAZ-WALLACE-LEOTA-
    CORONADO
LAWNRIDGE-ITASCA-EUSTIS-HUGHES-COLBY-BOAZ-
    WALLACE-LEOTA-CORONADO
RED CLOUD-PHILLIPSBURGH-TIFFANY-DIGHTON-SCOTT
    CITY-CORONADO
FORT SCOTT-IOLA-YATES CENTER-EL DORADO-
    NEWTON-LYONS-LYONS-GREAT BEND-NESS CITY-
    DIGHTON-SCOTT CITY-CORONADO
CORONADO OUTER SHELL
CORONADO DAY WAIT
CORONADO NIGHT WATCH
CORONADO BREACH
CORONADO INNER
```

It's a ghost town. I was little the first time I heard the term "ghost town"; I fell immediately in love. Coronado is still on all the maps, but to get there you'd have to crawl through Kansas forever. Still, if ever a testament is needed to the existence of the great fortress, the final stand, the place within which the search for some unnamed final shelter within the shelter would then begin and continue on forever and forever, it's here. This is what it looks like; these are its girders and panels. It is visible. It exists.

```
TRACE VISIBLE
TRACE NEARER
TRACE BREACH
```

15 When Tim from therapy started talking about board and care facilities, I was barely listening, but it turned out he wasn't just ticking off the options; that was actually the plan: every week there was a meeting called discharge conference, where my parents and I would sit down with my main doctor and one of the nurses and the therapist and the social worker, and we'd talk about how I was doing. The first discharge conference I attended had been the one where the doctor said: "Realistically, we don't know how long Sean will need to stay here." They hadn't thought I could hear them through the painkillers, but I could. For a long while after that, discharge conference was more of a weekly progress report, but eventually they'd start asking me questions: about my plans for after I left, about what would be different.

"Different?" I said. "Different how?"

The therapist spoke up. "Different, like how will you deal with frustration?"

I was still pretty foggy a lot of the time; I was heavily medicated. But I saw where she was going, what answer she was looking for. I kept looking at her in silence, because I didn't know what to say: it wasn't really a meaningful question to me. "What will you do when things don't go your way?" was the rephrasing she offered, meaning to clarify her point but just making it harder to explain that we were at odds in ways she wasn't likely to accept.

"Relaxation" was what I said, because Relaxation was one of the therapy groups I got wheeled to twice a week, and it was true that I found it useful; the group leader talked everybody through inner journeys to weird places, like a lake in the forest, and you were supposed to go there in your mind and feel at peace. It worked, in a way, though I always saw other things in the forest, which I kept to myself.

"Good," she said. "Thank you, Sean"; and so we moved on to the nurses, who talked about specifics of in-home aftercare, about having a night nurse at the very least in case of emergency, and asked my parents if they understood that changing dressings once a night was absolutely necessary for at least another twelve weeks, and so on. And then the conversation came around to someone I didn't know, dressed in street clothes with a name tag that said J. CAMPBELL / TRANSITIONAL LIVING.

I could tell from how he engaged my parents that they'd met before. I personally had never seen him. He didn't really ask questions; instead he gave a presentation about the place he worked. It had twenty-four beds, two to a room, and was for people who required various levels of care in transitioning from hospitals to—his phrase—*independent living*.

"After you turn eighteen, Sean," my mother said.

I soaked up the fluorescent light of the conference room and looked at everybody sitting around the table, people who'd seen all sorts of situations. I wasn't entirely sure what month it was anymore: were there eight months left before my birthday? Nine? I looked back at Mom, and I tried to think of a way to explain to her that I understood. That she was concerned for her son, hoping to do right by her son. But the picture she had of her son wasn't anyone still walking the earth: that was someone who had been destroyed. His life had been real once, and had value and meant something. But all that was gone now, remade in shapes and forms she hadn't come to understand just yet.

"It's OK, Mom," I said.

"I worry that you'll be lonely," she said; she was crying.

"I was going to be lonely anyway," I said, which I didn't mean to come out the way it did, but it did, and besides, it was true.

Lance took over the second letter from the newly formed alliance at about the halfway point, and Carrie never got it back. I'm pretty sure this was when I sort of let my guard down and let myself go, even though I knew better. Sometimes I guess you can't help yourself. By the time Lance's relentless scrawl started peaking at the end of the second page, he seemed to have forgotten that they were playing jointly; he talked about the interior of the game as if it were a place he'd escape from someday, and he wanted to remember to tell Carrie all about. *She will freak!* he said. *I know she will. But OK look. Before I leave these dead guys in the dust I am going to put a mark on their masks. Just write LANCE there aren't a lot of guys with my name anymore.*

You should avoid seeing too much of yourself anywhere: in the outside world, in others, in the imagined worlds that give you shelter. But I remembered Chris, who'd made it seem like it was safe, like it was OK once in a while. What harm was there, if things only happened in my mind? I had a moment's pause, though, about writing somebody's name on a mask that now concealed the face of a corpse. Lance's fever was infectious, a live virus, even through the page, even across the time that had elapsed between his stuffing it into an envelope and my opening it twenty-seven hundred miles away.

But I did it anyway—I wrote Lance's name on the mask; there was nothing to it. I drew a very crude picture of a supine body amid some broken boards, its masked face gazing out at the onlooker, LANCE on its forehead. The change was permanent for me; I didn't rewrite the turn, but it was always different afterward, even in the otherwise unremarkable year-plus between then and the week when I learned that they'd both gone off the grid. I couldn't remember a time when the body in the dust, whose presence compels the player to move on, hadn't had a name knifed into its mask. It gets hard to keep track of time, tracing back to someplace and trying to be diligent about it; and I don't even know why, really, I feel this drive for diligence or watchfulness, knowing already that there isn't anything worth finding at the beginning, nothing that points to anything. But I keep checking anyway. Just in case.

He ended the letter on a personal note, a tendency that persisted until the letters stopped coming. He told me about the town he lived in and what it was like in summer. *Kind of dead!* he said. *This is kind of the only thing there is to do around here, you ever feel like you're going crazy sometimes! This is kind of the only thing there is to do around here.* I had a terrible thought, which I am ashamed to have had, and which I will probably never be able to bring myself to write down.

Mom was crying again, trying to get my stuff together. It was time to go. They'd explained at the conference how I was going to need intensive treatment for at least the next year, and that it would be a while until they got a clear picture of how much reconstructive work would be possible. They talked about me, and my progress, in what was functionally the third person.

It had been the final discharge conference. I was leaving at five that afternoon; they were waiting to get some bloodwork back from the lab, stuff they technically needed to have on file in case anything happened to me later. I'd hurdled all the milestones for leaving weeks ago: I could walk steadily under my own power from a wheelchair to a bed; I could see clearly ahead of me, read an eye chart; my balance was improving. They'd fine-tuned the pain management profile so I could function while awake. The question of what exactly anybody was going to *do* with me remained.

A nurse's aide wheeled me down to the conference room, a corner room with big windows and white metal blinds tilted open. Mom and Dad were already there waiting, dressed a little better than they might otherwise have been; a doctor I was pretty sure I knew—there'd been a lot of them; I was still pretty foggy a lot of the time—explained why we were there, and then the questions started. The social worker asked variants on her how-do-you-plan-to-spend-your-time question; she was trying to assess risk, it seemed really obvious. "What are your outlets?" was the way she phrased it this time.

"Working on a game," I said.

"Good," she said. "What else can you do besides games?"

"I am making my own game," I said with some effort. I felt unexpected gratitude for the familiarity of the team. They understood me when I spoke. Outside of that small, exclusive club, no one would have been able to figure out what I was saying.

"For other people to play?" she said. I felt my vision making overtures toward the outside physical world, sensed the expanse of it. It felt unbelievably good.

"Yes," I said.

She raised her eyebrows and wrote something on the form she had on the table in front of her, nodding as she did so: not at me, but toward the nurses and the doctor. Then, still writing, not looking up: "What's changed since you came here?"

I thought hard; it was a good question. "I have bigger ideas," I said. I felt very smart and proud of myself for this answer. It was true, but loose.

"Better ideas about how to cope with situations?"

If I'd had any front teeth, I would have bitten my lower lip hard. You could hear, in the questions they asked and how they asked them, that there were right answers, things they wanted to hear. You could also, if you thought about it, understand that this was a preview of what the outside world was going to be like for the foreseeable future.

I weighed a few responses against one another in my head. There was a bargain to strike somewhere. You pick your battles. "Just bigger ideas," I said.

"What do you mean by 'bigger'?" she said.

I looked at everybody. I stopped caring about what they decided to do with me long enough to say *bigger* again, and then the doctor moved the conversation along, and I understood that all the decisions had actually already been made and this conference was only a formality.

My parents looked at the doctor; the doctor looked at me. The social worker looked down at her clipboard and shuffled a few papers from the bottom of her stack to the top, and she started in on Mom and Dad: Did they understood the options available to them? Did they know that if they chose to take me home the work would be hard, overwhelming sometimes? Had they done anything to make the house safer: What, specifically? "Specifically from my end," she said, looking directly at my mother, "have the guns been locked up?"

"There was only the one gun," my dad said.

I saw my mom holding herself with what still feels in memory like incredible dignity and grace. Her voice caught but she did not break. Things had been going on in the house while I'd been away, hard conversations.

"We got rid of it," she said. The social worker wrote something down. Dad took Mom's hand, there on top of the long table. The questions started up again. I looked out through the window at the road that led from hideous rooms like this to a safe refuge hidden deep in the ground somewhere in Kansas.

They had enclosed pictures of themselves, wallet-size portraits by a high school photographer. Lance was not a new player, but I felt that he was now starting off on a new adventure; I stopped to consider that, what it might mean for him. I guess no matter what your circumstances are you drift at some point from feeling like you're one of the young people to feeling like some of them could be your own kids. I hadn't noticed the drift; probably no one does: but I felt my eyes, where most of my expression is concentrated now, beginning to assume that hateful, condescending warmth you struggle your whole life to resist.

In his high school portrait Lance wore a crisp gray blazer; it felt like somebody'd picked it out for him, but it suited his expression, the very intentional seriousness he projected. It was a little big on him; I remembered my mother urging me to wear something nice on picture day every year, a sweet little memory. Lance's hair in the picture was long and thick, and you could see the fresh brushstrokes running through it where he or somebody else had put it into place just before the sitting. Curls bunched above his ears, playful intruders into the steely look he was trying to give the camera.

Carrie's picture was in softer light and was set before a cloudy-blue background screen. Her elbows rested on a shelf, and she looked like she was making an effort to hold the pose. Her hair was rusty blonde; it looked dry and brittle, and a little wild. She tried hard to meet the lens directly, but ended up looking like she was staring at something on the other side of it, maybe something way off in the distance: that blank stare people get when they're thinking too hard about how they're going to look. I looked at their pictures next to each other, nested against the chaotic give and take of their letter; their faces looked wet. My lips twitched. It was just lamplight on the gloss, of course, or something like that. I started to tell myself a story about it, and then I made a point of not taking the story any further, and I pulled an envelope from a drawer.

After the guy who invented Conan died a bunch of other people wrote Conan books. Some of them were by people who'd known him when he was alive; others were by fans who had their own ideas. I had a ton of these books. I could never get enough.

I wondered, in the privacy of my thoughts, whether the things that were interesting to me would leave me isolated at Transitional Living, but I didn't go to Transitional Living. We got as far as the walk-through and a final planning interview at the facility, and then we drove back to the hospital, we three together; there were two days left for me there, formalities. Blood tests, last visits, paperwork. I sensed the gravity of my position when we got back to my room.

"I don't want to go live with—with those people," I said after they'd brought me back to my room.

Dad looked at Mom, and Mom looked at me.

"We can't," my father said, "take care of you here. At-home here, back at the house. At home we can't take care of you."

"I know, Dad," I said. "I wonder if—"

I hadn't given any thought at all to what I was going to say.

"Your chair won't even fit in the main hallway," Dad said.

"We measured." I pictured Dad with his measuring tape in the hallway, Mom reading numbers to him. I could imagine the look on his face as he worked out numbers in his head, his lips moving maybe, simple math and its consequences. I wondered how much less I weighed now than I had a few months ago.

"I still get physical therapy after I leave," I said. "I'll be walking by myself after a while."

"By the time you're nineteen, Sean. They say you'll be walking unassisted when you're nineteen."

It would be a long time to keep me at home, I knew.

"If I can find a place to live by myself, will insurance pay?" I said. I had been around for enough insurance talk to understand that this was a big part of my future picture: who would pay for it. How I'd eat. When I asked this question, Dad looked at me like he was looking at a grown-up. I felt proud.

"They would," he said. "If you can find work, insurance will pay for your care, but otherwise you have to be at home for them to pay. I just can't see how you find a job with your—with your face—with your face like it is."

It was the first time either of them had said something so direct about how I looked, about how I was always going to look. Dad's little pausing stutter only slowed him down a little; I felt impressed with him, proud of him. I wanted to tell him. There was no way to tell him.

"I know I can figure something out if I can just have a little more time at home," I said, remembering my intensive care bed in the dark, the patterns in the ceiling, the infinity I'd learned I had in my head. I imagined a quiet future in an imaginary world where nothing ever really happened but everything seemed charged with life.

Mom looked at Dad; if she meant to convey any message to him in her look I couldn't read it.

"We can go home from here and talk about it for a while," Dad said after a long minute. "We don't have to decide anything today."

It was too quiet for everybody. Mom started gathering my books from the cheap nightstand with its floor-scraping wheels. *Conan the Freebooter. Conan of Aquilonia. Conan of the Red Brotherhood.*

Skulls in the Stars.

16

They're riding toward me now. They bear the mark of the captive on their forearms. These are men from a degraded oceanside kingdom somewhere far off, back where I come from, maybe: hunters with no personal interest in their bounty, conscripted into service by want or need. There're two of them; one gestures toward me, his finger arrow-straight in the oncoming Kansas dawn. He has seen the tangled mass of new growth on my chest. I'm standing there shirtless, wide open, all my weapons long since traded for food or medicine, corn-stubble on the hard winter earth, the thousand kings of the strewn territories as good as dead, drained, ad hoc leather cuffs tied to sticks swinging saddle-side. They're coming for me. There is an opening in the ground. I can stand and fight, or I can drop down. I have come too far to let myself be captured.

It was back when I was twenty-three, I think. Maybe twenty-two. From my own perspective my life was unremarkable. The pity strangers visibly felt for me, the unmistakable physical flinches they gave off on seeing me, were like map markings suggesting some present horror. But in my own eyes I was normal. Here and there, alone, reflecting, I'd bump up against what felt like a buffer zone between me and some vast reserve of grief, but its reinforcements were sturdy enough and its construction solid enough to prevent me from really ever smelling its air, feeling its wind on my face. There must be others like me who struggle more than I do. It makes me sad to think of them.

I got a phone call, anyway.

"A colleague of mine has been working on this new surgical technique people are having pretty good results with," said my old doctor. "He's had several patients, burn patients, you know, people with really significant trauma, and they've been able to live a, you know, a less secluded life."

I put on my glasses and I looked in the mirror.

Chris told me about the scalpel and the cyst as he prepared to launch an assault on the men in the gas masks by the overpass. Almost nobody began their play by attacking the cleanup guys; it was a nearly suicidal move. But Chris's involvement in the game, the intensity of it, was so total from the outset that it was hard to know what to think about it. I pictured him acting out his dreams in real space, pantomiming his moves in a room somewhere before he wrote them down. *I've got this cyst on my arm*, he wrote; *it's gonna be a problem but I grabbed a scalpel off a crashed ambulance when the fallout hit.* It was shocking stuff; this was his first full move.

I actually had a scalpel in the kitchen. I saw someone use

one on a cooking show once and it looked cool, and since I have to get gauze and Betadine from the medical supply store every so often, I'd picked one up the next time I went in. They didn't blink.

I used it once or twice to peel some oranges, and then I kept it on the desk for a while for opening letters. Using a scalpel to open my mail was a little more theatrical than I'd usually get in my daily life, the sort of thing people might imagine about me that wouldn't turn out to be true. But really it was an accident. It sounds sad to say "It gave me something to do," but it gave me something to do.

It's gone now, anyway. I sent it to Chris a few turns after he'd described his impromptu surgery. I ought not to have done this; I am pretty careful to avoid acting on the spur of the moment. But it felt like a fun and probably harmless improvisation, a tiny thing conceived of on a moment's notice. Still, I'd had to pack it up in bubble wrap, and find the right sort of box, and sending it required a trip to the post office instead of just placing a stuffed SASE in the mail slot on the door. That so much planning was necessarily involved is troubling to me; I don't like to think about it. *I can tell this is the wrong move I don't care!!* Chris had written at the end of that first turn. *I can't play through this with this burly knot on my arm!!!* And immediately, wide-eyed, I'd seen the playfield as it must have looked to him, really letting myself take in the full view of it through what felt like his eyes.

He never mentioned it again; I thought I understood why. It was a question of style. I put it, for the most part, out of my mind. Sometimes I'd remember when his turns would get long and intricate. *I get out the scalpel to kill snakes but there aren't any snakes actually in snake landing so I look pretty stupid*, he wrote once. No you don't, I thought before I could stop myself from thinking it. No you don't.

At home we worked out the mechanics of my situation, setting terms; my parents were very angry with me, and would stay angry for a long time. The air in the house would stink of blood forever; we'd breathe it as long as we lived there; new carpets didn't really help. There was nothing anybody could do about it now. Even if I could've explained myself, anything that felt like an overture toward pressing the issue was visibly too painful for them to stand.

I would take the California High School State Proficiency Exam; this was an important point to both of them. I would go to therapy weekly, all of it: physical therapy, talk therapy, the dermatologist. I'd talk to the job placement people whose contact information the social worker had sent home with the discharge papers, and if they found me work, I'd take it to save up money. Dad would work out my monthly payout with the insurance people and send it directly to me to help with rent once I'd found a place. I told them about the game I'd come up with in the hospital, how I thought it might bring in a few hundred dollars a month if people liked it; they didn't really try to hide their doubts, but they said that if it came to something, they'd support me in it. In a canvas tote from the hospital I had the papers I'd put together framing the full expanse of the Trace. They bulged in notebooks and folders that bore the hospital's name and its little futuristic logo, a stylized cross that doubled as a letter.

Over the course of the next month the house took on its own atmosphere, like a terrarium for fragile plants. I worked in earnest all day and into the night, sketching maps, writing turns. I stayed inside; the sun rising and setting outside my bedroom window became the sun of the Trace Italian, climbing the sky to illuminate the wasted plains of the near future, sinking down behind the western hills at night and leaving endless streaming dark in its wake. After I'd become adept with crutches, and later, when I walked, I'd go out to the front porch in the morning sometimes before the rest of the world was awake, thinking about the elaborate architecture of my invented world, how most of it lay east of here, in places I'd never see. Sometimes I'd turn my head left to look a little north, which always felt like the direction of the cold to me; ever since I was a kid and heard about the North Pole, where the snow never melted, I'd feel chills looking up toward Mount Baldy.

Chris followed a northward path when he first started playing. Lance and Carrie did the same thing a few years later. I took note of it at the time, but it was a connection I drew in the wrong place, like a surgeon putting an X on the wrong leg just before somebody fires up the saw.

I don't save everything. It would be impossible to save everything. From the busiest days of the game, starting in the summer of 1990, there's almost nothing left. Once I had boxes full of excited dispatches from across the country and occasionally even farther off: Mexico, Canada, Germany. But I cleaned and culled and thinned, and things lose meaning over time.

I grabbed a copy of *The Watchtower* from a small stack left on top of a *PennySaver* dispenser outside the Golden Arcade on the day of the accident, though, and I've saved it in a shoe box I keep near my desk. There's a story called "Who Hid the Dead Sea Scrolls?" in it. It has underlined phrases and half-sentences running through its three short paragraphs: *Sets out to reveal. Brought the bundles or sackfuls of texts from the capital to the desert caves for hiding. "All flesh is like grass, and all its glory is like a blossom of grass."* I don't remember reading it or underlining anything, which troubles me, which is sort of why I keep it.

I used to save these Xeroxed handbills some crazy person attached by thumbtack to local telephone poles warning about the imminent colonization of Earth by aliens; there's a few of these in the box, too, and some toys from the cheap toy dispensers you find in grocery stores. There are, finally, a few tapes, things a little too close to the bone for me to listen to but which I don't want to throw away; and a letter from Chris from right around when he started reaching depths I hadn't really foreseen. The turn he was answering had ended, *You see the horde of misshapen half-human creatures on bony horses. North toward Oregon they ride, always at night or in the waxing dusk, evading the hungry outsiders who kill horses for meat and their riders for sport. You see packs slung astride the horses. There's some brush just east.*

These guys can't touch me I'm going to live forever, Chris says toward the end of his second page, preparing to hurl himself upward and face-first toward the riders who weren't supposed to pose any threat, who had no designs on him down in the dirt in his overnight lair. I remember reading this letter and closing my eyes, both seeking out and fleeing from the sharp memory it called up, unable to decide where to go, where to put the parts of myself it seemed to make manifest in the room.

"It actually starts with tissue removal," he said, his voice getting livelier. "Because we—they—when you have a post-trauma reconstruction like the one you initially did, what they do is they take what's left and then reshape it, and they graft skin and in your case bone and that's how the reconstruction happens. But—and I don't know where you, what you—what your thoughts are about surgery."

I didn't remember much about the early surgeries.

"Well, we used to heavily favor what's called autografts, which is skin from the same patient, from somewhere else on your body. Or bone." I knew about this. "But we have synthetic polymers now. And the equipment's more accurate, which means we can work more quickly and get a much better result." He took a breath, and I took a breath.

"It's pretty dramatic," he said, "some of the results."

I was a little dazed; I usually start asking questions when I don't know what to say, so that's what I did. How many surgeries, how many sessions, how many times a week or month for how long.

"It varies," he said. "It's new. I don't want to say it's five sessions and then it turns out it's ten. Or more. But four or five is sort of the starting point, it's what we start out thinking about. It can be more. But it can be four, or five."

"And how much—"

"We think insurance will cover a fair bit of it. But because—"
When people break off I become immediately suspicious; I
was suspicious. "Because it would be valuable to my colleague
to practice his new technique, he thinks costs could be—"

This was a free shot.

"Well, we should meet up about it, anyway, sure," I said,
trying to sound as normal as I could: trying to make my reaction fit his expectations.

There was another little pause, a small emptiness, the distant sound of things he didn't quite want to tell me yet. Or
maybe not: I think sometimes I hear things as riddles that
aren't really riddles. "We should, yes," he said with that tone
of conclusion doctors get. "But if you're interested I'd like to
go ahead and schedule the first procedure, just to get you in
there. It'll take a few weeks to get the approvals process rolling. When surgeries are new the paperwork's heavier. It won't
be much at all on your end, just a lot here in the office, but if
we schedule it now we'll be able to put the whole thing in
motion."

I said, "All right," and he said, "Great," but I had managed
to do quite a bit of thinking between phrases, to look into
various futures and think just enough about them to know if I
liked them or not. I remembered the lights of the ambulance
and the sound of the voices yelling. The chaos. The involun-
tary twitching in my toes, and the raw, open feeling all over my
face. And then he said I should call the main office to make an
appointment and to mention his name when I did, and that
they'd "get me right in." And he gave me the number, and I
repeated it slowly as he went, doing my best to pretend I was
writing it down.

Somebody'd parked a truck out in front with the windows down and the radio playing. It was really loud. The music was in Spanish so I couldn't understand it; I only ever took one semester of Spanish and that was in the seventh grade. Sometimes if outside noise starts to bother me I'll put some music on inside the house to blanket it over, or I'll go to the park and feed squirrels, or maybe go get candy and hope it's quieter when I come back. But for some reason I can't pin down, I had a weird feeling of attachment to the music from the truck out by the curb. It wasn't an intrusion; it belonged.

The driver was still in the cab: I saw him from my window. I was standing there taking in the early-morning breeze, these winds that're native to Southern California, Santa Anas. They make the brush fires worse. His radio'd jolted me awake, but I didn't really mind. He wasn't singing along or nodding his head back and forth or smoking a cigarette or anything. He was sitting there staring straight ahead. Waiting for somebody, I guess. He was wearing some kind of work jumpsuit, like the guys at the auto shop wear, dull dark blue.

I had this rising premonition about him turning to look over at me, catching me in the act of sort of staring at him for no reason. It was a premonition with texture and heft, something I could almost taste; in my mind I saw his head begin to turn, casually, gradually but decisively, until his eyes found mine and held them. I stood ready for this to happen, wondering what I'd do, but he stayed put. He listened to the Spanish music and gazed out at the road ahead of him, steady through the windshield, and I got so worried he'd catch me that I began faking movements, pretending to survey the rest of my out-look in a broad sweep from right to left: the front walkway, the hedges, the street. When I swiveled my gaze back toward him he was starting up the truck.

I expected he'd just leave then, because it always seems to me like nothing ever happens, but something did happen: he began to back up. Monte Vista's a busy street during the day-time, but it was too early for traffic and there wasn't anybody parked in front of him, so I couldn't figure out what he was doing. He checked the rearview very intently, his neck rigid, head still like a hawk, and then I realized, quickly, that he was accelerating in reverse, that there was another car parked be-hind his with enough gap between them to allow him to build up some speed.

The next minute—it couldn't have been longer than a minute—went predictably: the gunning motor, the artificial thunder-crack of the crashing fenders, and then the fallout: things dropping from the cars' frames to the asphalt, making *ping* sounds when they hit. In a movie version of this scene the driver wheels his glance abruptly to the window where a mis-shapen man stands watching it all unfold, and fixes me with a threatening look. That didn't happen. He braced himself hard just before the collision, and after it he spent maybe fifteen seconds looking over his shoulder, surveying the damage as best he could from his restricted vantage point. Then he looked back into the rearview to check for cars. There weren't any, so he shifted into drive and headed north, at a clip but not speed-ing away, eyes forward, his hands at ten and two.

Once he was gone you would have had to've stopped and looked around to know anything had happened. There was a good chance that the driver of the car he'd rammed wouldn't notice he'd been hit for a day or two: if he came up to the driver's side door from behind, he might not see anything. I thought about the guy in the truck, the focus in his expression, and I felt like I already knew enough of the story to tell it to somebody else maybe better than either of its major players could. But I didn't call the police, even though I know you're supposed to. And I hadn't taken any notice of the guy's license plate, or written down any of the details. I'd answer questions about what I'd seen if anybody asked me, but I know what I know. Nobody was going to ask. So I just stood there at the window for a minute more, and I heard a bird singing; and while I am a person who, for reasons I consider good, am reluctant to assign specific meaning to anything I see or hear going on out there in the natural world, I couldn't get out of the way of a sort of prophetic feeling I assume everyone gets from time to time. I couldn't see the bird, I didn't know where it was; I told myself a few stories about it, how it was a migratory bird I'd happened to catch on just the right morning, separated from its company en route to cooler days; or again how it was dying, singing some cheerful dying song. Kids' stuff, old stuff. And then I had a memory from childhood, not childhood really but a while afterward, but what felt, in that moment, like childhood.

17

It was JJ; Teague; Tara, who was JJ's girlfriend; Kimmy, who was Tara's friend; and then me. It was the middle of the week. We were bored, sitting around on the aluminum bleachers up by the practice baseball diamond on the other side of the high school parking lot, waiting for something to happen. Tara had her boom box and we were listening to *Relayer*. I was looking hard at the tape shell and thinking the thoughts I get looking at tape shells. Am I the only person who gets the hard creeps from this guy's face? was what I was thinking specifically. I was looking at the singer from Yes. His mouth looked like it was from somebody else's head. I couldn't make all the pieces fit.

Teague was teaching himself to dungeon master; he'd gotten *The Dungeon Master's Guide* from his parents for Christmas. It was May now. You could see from the book he'd already read it a million times. The front was like a wrinkled old map, and half the pages were bent in at the corners. He was hunched over it with his index finger pointing at the middle of a page and his eyebrows scrunched down. When Teague is irritated it's really obvious.

"Can we listen to some Rush?" he said without looking up.

The Yes tape was Kimmy's but she had all kinds of different music so she started digging through her gigantic purse to try to find something else to play. In her purse, tape shells clacked against one another while she dug; you could hear them scraping against each other, against keys, against pens and compacts, the sounds muffled in the purse's puffy vinyl folds. To me it sounded like somebody shaking up dry bones. I closed my eyes and thought about those old bones in some girl's purse and then I let my mind go: if you wanted to fit bones into your purse they'd have to be broken into pieces; you couldn't fit a whole arm bone or a leg bone or a skull in there, just teeth, toes, and fingers; maybe kneecaps; but my imagination told me teeth would make a high sound, like pieces of glass, and toes would sound dull, like old crushed cans. That left fingers. I remembered biology class when we did anatomy. Distal phalanges, proximal phalanges, metacarpals. To walk around with a bag full of bones in the normal world would require a stone constitution. You could be a thief. You could be an actor, probably. Actors die young in ancient Rome, though. If it's the present day and you're Kimmy, and you're carrying someone's bones around in your purse, then I have a lot of questions for you, and I'll probably never ask them, and you'll have a secret that only I have guessed.

When I snapped out of it Kimmy'd popped out Yes and put in *2112*. She has everything. JJ and Tara were halfway making out. She had her hand on his pants, moving up the thigh. He was two years older than her, already out of high school.

Nobody really knew what he was doing with his life, because we only ever saw him at the park when he wanted to hang out with Tara. He had a mustache.

I was ditching P.E. to come up and hang out with everybody. I started to worry that if I missed two classes the school might call my house, and I'd get in trouble, and when I start to worry I can't stop, so I told everybody "Later." I felt sad to leave even though there was nothing going on. The sun was out and it was really bright; I wished I had some sunglasses. I walked across the parking lot toward the school, and then somebody honked at me. I never look up when people honk at me because I don't want any trouble. People gave me trouble back then because of the way I dressed and because they didn't like my friends. Inside I hated anybody who honked at me and wished I could cause their car to crash using only the powers of my mind. I could see what the crashes would look like from the outside and what they would feel like inside the car. It was awesome.

I once heard in a science class that you don't start remembering things until you're three, or maybe five. When I remember this day and most things before it, it's like trying to remember being four years old, or two. I can see it, and I know it happened, and I have enough information about it to reconstruct the whole scene to my own satisfaction, but the person to whom it happened is somewhere so far off that I only know it's me because I can see his face, and because I'm the one remembering.

Later that day I walked home in the bright sun. I remember seeing the bottlebrush bushes that lined the street for the last

189

four blocks, how they looked ancient, or maybe Martian. Alien. Home from school was a straight shot through four different neighborhoods, and by the time I got home, I always felt like a traveler returning from a great journey, relearning what home was like, acclimating to newly unfamiliar waters. Two packages were waiting for me on the front porch; I was glad to get to them first, because sometimes my parents teased me about how much time I spent with my books and tapes and magazines. Or they tried to start conversations about what I was into. I hated that. It wasn't like with some of my other friends, whose parents were Christians; my parents weren't Christian like that. But they did say they "wondered about where I was headed." That was how they put it. It got on my nerves. So if I sent off for something cool, I avoided opening it in front of them. I didn't want to have to answer any questions.

I went back to my room and spread the mail out on my bed. One of the packages was from Brazil: it was a sword catalog. I'd seen an ad for it in one of the little magazines I got at the game store. It cost three dollars, but mail from far away was worth a little extra, so I hid three ones inside a folded piece of newspaper and sent it off to São Paulo. *Catalog of Rare and Unknown Swords from Around the World, Send Three Dollars and Two International Reply Coupons.* It was like a treasure to me, weird alphabet letters in the return address and a strange slick sheen to the envelope. Sometimes when you send off for something without knowing what it is, what you get back looks like a third-generation copy somebody found somewhere, but this was nice: glossy paper, clean staples. Some of the swords had hilts with designs, like dragons or horses, and some had what looked like jewels. *Smooth semi-precious stones inlaid afford textured grip.* The prices were listed in a currency I'd never heard of; it had a little symbol that set my mind racing to the good places.

The other package was from up north in Oregon, some town I'd never heard of before, Grants Pass. It was a membership patch from Inter-Hyborea, a Conan fan club; it came with a tape of songs based on Conan stories. The patch was high quality and was going to look very cool on my backpack if I could just get it on there without getting caught. This was going to involve a needle and thread and working on the patch in secret, or asking a girl to do it for me. If I asked Tara, JJ would be mad, but Kimmy was a possibility so I called her. I had my own phone in the room ever since Christmas, because if they didn't give me my own phone I'd always be in the living room talking and no one would be able to hear the TV. It was a good deal.

Kimmy either didn't believe I couldn't sew the patch on myself or she just wanted to tease me; she pretended she didn't understand what I was asking, and then either she pretended she thought the patch was an excuse for me to come over to her place or she actually believed that. It made me mad, and I felt embarrassed, and the conversation gradually evaporated until neither one of us was saying anything. Then her voice got softer and friendlier, and she said everybody knew how to sew. But actually I didn't know any guys who took sewing. It was the least popular elective class for guys, below even accounting. So I made a joke out of it, and said during registration I tried to sign up for sewing but all the jocks beat me to it. That was a joke for us to share, because I hated all sports, and she hated guys on the football team specifically; I didn't know why specifically the football team. I didn't care. I hated them, too.

Then she said when did I want to get the patch sewn on, and I felt so good, because our group of friends was so tight. We helped each other. It was like we had a code, a way of doing things. A way we treated each other. I'd known when I'd picked up the phone to call her that she would eventually say yes to sewing on my patch, but she'd give me a hard time first, and if I stuck with it and stayed cool, it would all turn out nice. And that was exactly how it happened. There was for me in that time a real comfort in feeling a sort of casual ability to predict the future.

I said I could probably come over later that evening, and she said: "You're so lucky you have cool parents," and I pictured my parents: how they looked at me now that my hair was long, how they looked at each other a lot when they were talking to me. How obvious it seemed to me that somewhere along the line our paths had forked, and now we were on different tracks looking at each other across a distance that would soon be infinite. Cool parents, I thought, are the ones who know nothing. It made me feel a little sad for mine, but I didn't say any of this. I had a funny feeling that day, all day: something about how much I liked my life and where I was with it.

So I told Kimmy I would come over at seven. She said, "If I sew your patch on you owe me." And I said, OK, cool, I'll see you there.

Lying on my bed, I listened to the Conan tape on my tiny cassette radio. There were ten songs by ten different bands or people on it, nobody I'd ever heard of. Some were just guys with acoustic guitars telling stories and some were bands with loud guitars and maybe a violin in there howling and squealing away. One was just a guy playing an organ with no singing at all. Mostly it sounded very cheap, but some of them were trying very hard to make something that sounded majestic and mighty. I loved it; nobody I knew listened to stuff like this. I looked at the tape shell, trying to think about all these people I didn't know anything about from somewhere way up north, making music for people who cared about Conan. And I picked one of them at random to make a little mini-poster for, a band called Crom.

First I drew a picture of a skull, and then I put a helmet with horns over the skull. Then I put little flames inside the eye sockets. You couldn't really see the flames unless you were looking for them. I did the whole thing with a mechanical pencil, and when I looked at the flames, they were still too clear; I wanted the eyes sitting way back, so they looked out from somewhere so far inside that looking into them would require real concentration and effort. I tried different shapes for the flames, first rounder and softer and then little pyramids almost, and then I went with little diamonds instead. You could only see the diamonds if you leaned in super close. The sockets were otherwise completely black.

At the table, Mom asked what I'd been drawing when she came to get me for dinner, and I pretended I didn't know what she was talking about. It was like walking a tightrope. I'd been lying on my bed with the sketchbook open and several different pencils at hand for different shadings, and she'd knocked once and then opened the door; as soon as I'd heard the knock, reflexively I closed my notebook, just to be safe, I'm not sure from what, but I was still there with a notebook in front of me when she came in.

"The thing you were drawing, just now, when I came to get you."

"I can't draw," I said.

"But you were drawing something, weren't you? When I came in, just now," she said.

"Not really," I said. There are planets so far away from ours that no scientist will ever guess that they exist, let alone know the stories of their civilizations, their beginnings and ends. They're not being kept secret from us, but they're secret all the same.

"All right," said Mom, looking over at my father for support, but he wasn't paying attention. The TV was on in the living room, and he had a sight line to it from his chair. He was watching the news. I didn't know why my dad liked to watch the news, because it made him angry, and the angrier he got, the louder he'd have to turn up the volume to hear the news over the things he yelled back at it. It got louder over the space of two hours most nights, and then the news was over. This made the house during dinnertime feel like an insane asylum.

Every night now there was new stuff about Libya. The *CBS Evening News* would show short clips of Gadhafi, who was president of Libya, or king, it was never clear to me. He was usually in sunglasses. Sometimes he'd be wearing a weird scarf bunched up around his neck, sailing out on the open sea somewhere maybe, or else riding around the streets in a military van. Everyone around him would always be smiling and sometimes yelling. You couldn't see his eyes through the lenses, so it was hard to say what was going on in his head, but I always imagined he felt good. He looked like a white point in a map of a moving weather system. Cameras pointing at him, people yelling questions constantly, and him just standing amid it all holding his head still, waiting to see what he had to say, and sometimes speaking, subtitles quietly translating on the screen.

My father hated him; a bomb had gone off in the Vienna airport at Christmas, and the story'd been on the news every day for a week. Mom and Dad had gone to Vienna for vacation once before I was born, so for my dad this made the whole thing personal. He'd try to explain the stories to me as they ran, to get me excited about them like he was: and I'd try; I'd nod and pay close attention as his voice rose. But I couldn't make myself care much about it: it seemed like nothing; I couldn't keep any of it straight. The jagged, blurry pieces of footage spoke to me a little; there was something in them like a code or a secret message, not for me necessarily but for somebody. Or maybe for nobody, but hidden there all the same. But I didn't know how to steer the conversation that way, or what I'd say about it if I succeeded.

We were having meat loaf with tomato sauce. I didn't like meat loaf, but my mother remembered that I'd loved it as a kid. If I ate too slowly she'd say: "You used to love meat loaf!" I never knew what to say back, though that night I tried "It's good" while stuffing a forkful of peas, potatoes, and meat loaf all into my mouth at once. I tried to remember liking meat loaf as a kid; for my mother the memory was so vivid she couldn't forget it, but I couldn't remember anything about it. At all. I knew we'd eaten it a lot, because you could make a pound of meat last longer by making meat loaf with it, but the only taste I could think of was the one I was trying to mask by eating everything on my plate at once. It was sad. "I like the sauce," I tried again.

Then the story on gas prices came to an end, and they started in on Gadhafi. It had something to do with ships in foreign waters. "American ships in Libyan waters" was how it started off, and that was all I really heard: everything else receded quickly into the background for me and became nothing within a few seconds. Libyan waters. Dad watched while he ate and Mom watched his face nervously, and I wondered to myself whether waters take on special qualities depending on who they belong to.

I went out on a limb.

"Dad," I said when the commercial started up, "are Libyan waters different from other waters?"

"Sean," said Mom.

"They're different because of sovereignty," he said, keeping his eyes on his plate.

"Bill," said Mom.

"But there aren't any actual lines on the water or anything," I said.

"They have maps and coordinates," my dad said.

"Right, but the water—"

"The water is the same," said my dad.

I stopped. There were a lot of things I might have said to

either make the conversation worse or move it off in some different direction, but I liked where it rested as I spun: out in international waters with imaginary lines on their surface that no one could actually see.

You can't see the hall closet from the dinner table, so I excused myself a couple of minutes early. Mom asked if I'd be back for dessert just as I turned the corner out of sight. When I got back to my room, I slid the rifle and the ammo under my bed, and I put on a Robin Trower record: *Bridge of Sighs*. I'd bought it in the twenty-five-cent bin with my allowance one week a long time ago, sixth grade maybe. Back then I'd gotten really into it, because I was the only person I knew who'd ever heard of it; nobody listened to Robin Trower. I knew his name from seeing his picture in *Hit Parader* once or twice. But I'd only ended up with the record by accident, because the name sounded cool and the cover looked weird and I had a dollar in my pocket and it only cost a quarter. I didn't understand it, really, because without the context of other people's thoughts on it, it couldn't really find steady footing in my mind. I wrote his name on my jeans at one point anyway, just to see how it felt: ROBIN TROWER right there on my knee. I outgrew the jeans before it washed out.

In my mind the singer was looking me right in my eyes while he sang. Then he had his hands on my shoulders. Then he was shaking me. I had made up a face and clothes for him, to imagine what he looked like: the album cover was just a swirling white design with words in twisting, curling letters on it, no pictures. I pictured the singer with long hair, big strong hands, wide shoulders, and a blue suit that fit him loosely. I put my head about an inch in front of the speakers, right between them, and I closed my eyes. He sang: "Living in the day of the eagle, the eagle not the dove." It sounded like he was making up the words as he went along, reacting to a story in his mind as he watched it develop, because he stopped in the middle of the sentence. Right after *not the*. I liked it, because it was how I felt: not knowing what to say but wanting to say something. Saying something anyway because your mouth just keeps moving and the rhythm is behind you and you can't stop. The eagle, not the . . . dove. And then the song went into the slow part, and I began to drift.

Kimmy was out in front of her house when I got there. I heard background music as I drew closer to her; I could picture the street and the lawn and the back of my head, the broader view. Everything on a screen. When she saw me coming, she walked out to the middle of the street and said: "Let's go"—I wasn't sure if she put it like that because we were supposed to be getting away from somebody, possibly her parents, so I just went along. The plan had been to study at her place, so I asked what was up, and she said she'd tell me later but right now we should probably go someplace like to the arcade. I never found out why we couldn't go inside. "I'll tell you later" is a contingent claim that can be rendered false by any of several moves.

On the way to the arcade she pulled a pack of Marlboro 100s out of her puffy vest and offered me one. Most of my friends smoked now, but I usually didn't. I took one anyway, and as we walked I took tiny puffs so I wouldn't cough. Kimmy asked if I was going to be around this summer, and I said, "I'm always around," which sounded terrible to me, like I didn't have any real life at all. She was going to Oregon to stay with her mom for at least two weeks. My family had vacation in the summer, too, when Dad took two weeks off work, but we never went anywhere: we stayed home and took long drives, or swam at the hotel pool down the street. It was all right, but every year I felt a little more like I'd never seen anything, like I'd missed out on the stuff my friends kept getting every time school let out.

The arcade was next to a liquor store about six blocks up Monte Vista. It was called Golden Arcade and nobody ever went there. The cool arcade was Starship over in Upland, next to Pic 'n Save: it had an entrance built to look like a spaceship hatch, and blue track lighting all up and down the walkways inside. It had two levels and six walls, and you could get lost in there, or find things you'd missed every other time you'd gone in. But it would have taken us two hours to walk to Starship, and that was OK, because there were always people there from other schools anyway, and I was always afraid of people my age from other schools. They made me tense. But there was never anybody at Golden Arcade except the woman who worked there. She sat behind a counter listening to a small radio, reading a magazine, waiting for customers who never came. I don't think she even saw us come through the door.

They didn't have too many new games there but the ones they had were super clean, and you could see them all from where you stood as soon as you walked in: the arcade was a single rectangular room with games pushed back up against three of the walls and two air hockey tables in the middle. The air hockey tables gave off a loud, cold hum. Kimmy strolled from machine to machine while I got quarters, and then she stopped at Xevious, which is what you play when you get tired of all the popular games. Xevious was mainly gray and soft black, and had music like a lullaby, and everything in it seemed to happen in slow motion. Once when my mom asked me why I liked to play video games I said it was because they were relaxing, and she looked at me like I'd sprouted horns, but Xevious is a very relaxing game. Playing it was like watching flowers bloom. Weird metal airplanes flew over the green and gray background dropping bombs on everything, explosions splashing like soft cymbals, and your only targets were buildings. If there was anybody in the buildings you never saw them go in or out. It was like strafing an abandoned city in an ever-climbing vertical scroll.

We played doubles. I lost. It was a good time, and then after we'd played all our quarters, we went out behind the building to smoke more cigarettes and she asked me if I believed in God. I didn't have any idea why she was asking but that was something I had always liked about her. She talked about everything.

I was about to make something up about God being an alien consciousness, not even human, because in junior high I worked out a theory about that once during science class. But I had an urge to be as honest with Kimmy as I could. I told her I thought God was just your dad. Like when you grew up and weren't afraid of your dad anymore you got God instead, and you could make him whatever you wanted.

"You don't believe in Jesus?" she said.

I said, "I don't know," which was kind of true. When people said *Jesus* it still always sounded to me like it had to mean something special. Different from other words. I knew I didn't believe what Christians believed, about how if you said the name you would be saved. Saved from what? But still, when anybody said it, when you heard it out loud, something always seemed to happen. A shift in the light. Something about perspective. No matter how quiet they said it or whether they kept talking, it changed everything for a few minutes.

So I knew I believed something about Jesus, but I wasn't sure what it was, or why she was asking. Kimmy said: "I believe Jesus is Lord," and I knew this was a signal, a way of opening a path for us into something private and shared. And for a split second, whose limits lie out past the farthest reaches of the universe, I contemplated letting her into the dark, distant corners where Conan grew cruel and lived inside me, where I became a person with the power to blind strangers with a single gesture, where the dull edges of my life grew sharp enough to cut through rock. But instead I kissed her, and she kissed me back, with her tongue. We kept going like this for five or ten minutes and then without looking down she took my right hand in her left and guided it down the front of her jeans.

People were always saying how ugly Southern California was, especially when they came back from their summer vacations. They said it looked plastic or fake or whatever, and talked about all the cool things they saw in Ohio, where their grandparents lived. Or in Pennsylvania. The wall behind the arcade was made of giant sparkling white bricks, just like all the other buildings connected to it. There was graffiti on it, indecipherable gang writing. It was dark now and getting a little cold and then the super-bright lights they have behind stores to keep bums from sleeping by the dumpsters came on, and I thought, people who don't think Southern California is the most beautiful place in the world are idiots and I hope they choke on their tongues.

Mom was in her purple nightgown when I got home. It was about 9:30. There was another TV in the bedroom and Dad was back there watching. I could hear it. Mom asked how studying went and I said, "Great," and she asked what we studied and I said, "American history." She told a story about her history teacher in high school, and my head was so full of other stuff it was hard to listen, even though it wasn't like I didn't care. But I had to struggle to pay attention.

"What have you got there?" she said.

"One of those free magazines," I said. I handed it to her. She looked at the cover, her eyes sleepy but focusing hard.

" 'Who Hid the Dead Sea Scrolls?' " she said. "Jehovah's Witnesses?"

"I guess," I said.

"Are you going to join up with the Jehovah's Witnesses?" she said. I couldn't tell if she was teasing, or just talking like you do when you get too tired, or if she was trying to see what was up with me. She was asking a lot of questions lately. I felt one of those urges I always got when I was younger and that I still get sometimes: to just say something for the explicit purpose of blasting a hole through the conversation. *We're all witnesses except me. I'm an unaligned cleric.* She leafed through the pages.

"The picture on the front, I just liked it," I said. "And the Dead Sea."

"'Its glory is like a blossom of grass,'" she read from *The Watchtower*, which I must have underlined sometime during the next hour or two, possibly, I'm not sure; as I say it's possible the underlining was already in there when I picked it up, I don't remember.

Later, when it was late, I thought about taking out the whole house at once, and I rode that idea like a wave for ten or fifteen minutes; everybody was asleep, if I was quick nobody'd even have time to feel afraid or confused. I was a good shot, I could make it painless. How long would I stand, a new creation, blood-flecked and alone in the noiseless dark? The police would find me standing silently there, motionless, waiting for them to take their turn. There, at the far end of the hall with their pistols raised, commands I'd never hear issuing fruitlessly from their straining jaws, their voices lost in the all-consuming quiet . . . *Whose uniforms are those? Who do you represent?* I got as far as the door to my parents' room and I stood outside it, stock in hand. My breathing was shallow now; I heard it whistling from my nose and I felt the rifle stock rising, falling, rising, gently, evenly, barely perceptible except yes, as my shoulder followed the expanse and descent of my chest. All stillnesses amplified to a tritone hum. I contemplated my mission there, right on the threshold, but all honor had gone missing from it, too many threads came loose and couldn't be drawn back in. And so I thought about what was important to me: about how I would want to be remembered, about the totality of my vision realizing itself now under the heavy pressure of the moment but remaining true, still true, to the impermeable solitude of its origins.

And I remembered Conan, the real one: how he conquered with honor, how his code cohered. People don't usually understand this when I try to explain it, which is why I've stopped trying, nor will never try again, no, not in courtrooms nor in conferences: but when it came down to the actual moment, I was trying to make the right decision. I can never trace all the paths back to it clearly enough to know for sure if I did, or not; I know there must be other navigable paths where either nothing happens, that night or later, or where, when the idea to just pull the curtain on most things and then on everything *just because* crosses my mind, I let the moment pass, and I go to sleep like everybody else did on my street that night. I finally get my own car, and I graduate with my class, and eventually I either go to college or get a job, and somewhere off in the hidden gullies of the future I'm a good dad to a kid who looks like I did when I was small. How his grandparents beam. Or maybe instead I just stay up in my room, picking out swords from the Brazilian catalog, and I send off for them, only then two weeks later they're here, the falchion blunt in its aspect like a hand-hewn machete, and the great Sword of Attila, dull golden horns sprouting from the head at its hilt and blank dead empty eye sockets pinkie-wide in the bulging forged face beneath, hollow negative space palpable when I close my palm around the hilt and head out into the moonlight, naked to the waist, going house to house, gore streaming from my blade as I emerge: my blade Who in its infinite mercy leaves no sign of its passing on those whom it favors, yet woe, woe to those in whom no favor is found; or maybe I get the swords, but then I just hang them on the wall, and there they sit, mute, domesticated, blameless, and years later Mom calls: "What do you want me to do with these swords, you left them in your room when you moved out, if you want I can put them in the garage sale," and I tell her she can do whatever she wants with them; I'm a different person now. I saw it then briefly, and I see it clearly now, but these possibilities are lost in the play, hidden somewhere in the hills of Hyborea, diamonds stuffed into the hollows of stripped skulls and spirited by night into a far corner of a distant cave above the plains where I *drank in the lush vistas of the inner gardens, seen by no one, clear to no eye. The pulsing bare light in which they grew, its dull glow eternal, originating who knew where, pale and diffuse. Wild tendrils seeking the outer walls of the circular room, climbing the Plexiglas toward no light. Behind me the titanium door auto-locked; a cool mist began to drift from somewhere in the latticework. All at once the air hissed: first within, and then from the halls beyond. I heard the voices of the guards, their code language cracking in desperation. They were kicking at the door. But the inner gardens, made safe centuries ago for no recorded purpose, can only be entered at the appointed hour. For days I would plot my escape, breathing clean air, consulting the illustrated booklet about edible plants I'd gotten in trade for bullets.*

There was a summer-long gap between me and all the stuff that was supposed to happen next; I now saw, nested within that gap, possibilities without number. Infinite futures. I am a musician on a stage somewhere, my instrument singing in tones so universal that the masses howl their accord in places near and far: Reseda, New York, Japan; or else I escape through a bedroom window three minutes from now and careen through the streets, crazed, lost, locked inside the person in whose image I have remade myself; or I am no one, driving a delivery van carrying boxes of electronics from nowhere to no place, the road empty before me by day, shared by headless headlights after dark, beams increasing briefly and then gone, beyond, somewhere off in the cross-traffic, catchable in the rearview if I dare. I thrive. I fail to thrive. I fall. I rise. Too many. Too late. Not that, not those, not these: *this*.

I treaded the carpet backwards from my parents' door, alone and awake, and I caught sight of the painting of the cowboys at sunset, smoke rising from their campfire in the foothills, black and even as it sought the coming darkness. I could hear my heart beating in my ears. I waved at the cowboys, and then one waved back at me, a faint movement in the dark orange glow of his eternal sunset, imagine that, for just one second the glint of his tin cup, the smell of his drying skin at day's end, head turning now back to the fire and its permanent smudging blur. And then I went back into my room, locked into a sequence as perfect as a pattern, and I sat down on my great rock throne, invisible to the outside world but palpable beneath me, and from how my face felt I thought maybe I was crying, either because I didn't want to do this or because I did, it was hard to tell and anyway I never would, who would believe me in either case and who would be there to believe me in all cases, it was a puzzle, I had yet to learn the way of the jigsaw, and so I positioned the rifle beneath my chin, it feels cold, like an actual thing in the actual present physical world, OK, there it is, I am here now, and then I *lay down on my belly and listened to the rising squall beyond the door.*

Acknowledgments

For their generous ears, watchful eyes, and great suggestions,
deepest gratitude to:

CHRIS PARRIS-LAMB

SEAN MCDONALD

LALITREE AND ROMAN DARNIELLE

TAYLOR SPERRY

LENNI WOLFF

A Note About the Author

John Darnielle is a writer, composer, guitarist, and vocalist for the band the Mountain Goats; he is widely considered one of the best lyricists of his generation. He lives in Durham, North Carolina, with his wife and son.